PAPERCUTZ™

NANCY DREW
girl detective®

Graphic Novels available from Papercutz
$7.95 each in paperback, $12.95 each in hardcover.
Please add $3.00 for postage and handling for the first book, add $1.00 for each additional book.

Send for our catalog:
Papercutz
40 Exchange Place, Suite 1308
New York, NY 10005
www.papercutz.com

Graphic Novel #1
"The Demon of River Heights"

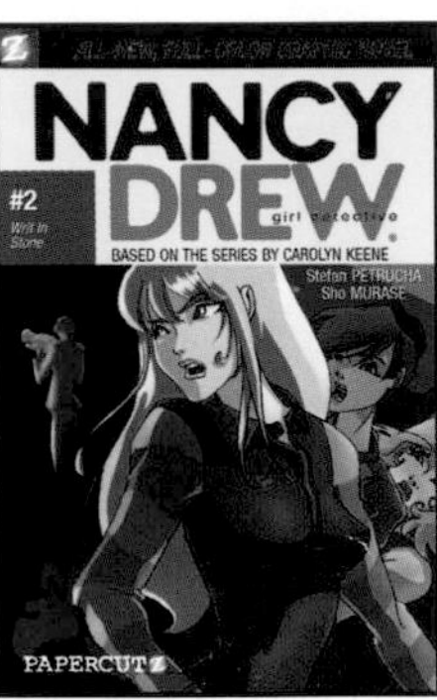

Graphic Novel #2
"Writ In Stone"

Graphic Novel #3
"The Haunted Dollhouse"

Graphic Novel #4
"The Girl Who Wasn't Ther

Graphic Novel #5
"The Fake Heir"

Graphic Novel #6
"Mr. Cheeters Is Missing"

Coming in November
Graphic Novel #7
"The Charmed Bracelet"

NANCY DREW

#5 girl detective®

The Fake Heir

STEFAN PETRUCHA • Writer

DANIEL VAUGHN ROSS • Artist

with 3D CG elements by LUIS LUNDGREN

Cover, preview pages, and art direction by SHO MURASE

Based on the series by

CAROLYN KEENE

New York

The Fake Heir
STEFAN PETRUCHA – Writer
DANIEL VAUGHN ROSS – Artist
with 3D CG elements by LUIS LUNDGREN
BRYAN SENKA – Letterer
CARLOS JOSE GUZMAN – Colorist
JIM SALICRUP
Editor-in-Chief

Nancy Drew volunteers with Project Sunshine.
Project Sunshine is a nonprofit organization that provides free services to children and families affected by medical challenges. We send volunteers to hospitals to provide arts and crafts, tutoring and other special services. For more information on Project Sunshine please visit www.projectsunshine.org.

ISBN 10: 1-59707-060-2 paperback edition
ISBN 13: 978-1-59707-060-7 paperback edition

Printed in China.

10 9 8 7 6 5 4 3 2

NANCY DREW, GIRL DETECTIVE HERE. FOR A CHANGE, I'M TAKING A DAY OFF.
PERSONALLY, I DIDN'T THINK I NEEDED A DAY OFF. I LOVE MYSTERIES! CAN'T GET ENOUGH OF THEM.
BUT WHEN MY BEST FRIEND BESS GOT AN OFFER TO SPEND THE DAY ON A SAILBOAT, A FEW PEOPLE SORT OF INSISTED I SHOULD.
A FEW PEOPLE INCLUDING MY DAD, CARSON DREW, MY HOUSEKEEPER HANNAH, MY BOYFRIEND, NED, MY OTHER BEST FRIEND, GEORGE AND...
WELL, EVERYONE I KNOW, REALLY.
BUT SOMETIMES EVEN WHEN I'M NOT LOOKING FOR MYSTERIES, THEY COME TO ME.
CHAPTER ONE: A BREAK AT THE LAKE

GREET-INGS BLAND BLONDE AND HANGERS-ON!
THOUGHT I'D COME BY TO MAKE YOU JEALOUS OF THE FACT THAT MY DAD JUST BOUGHT A NEW LAKESIDE CABIN!
D.D
SAY, WHAT'S THAT UGLY BUMP ON THE JET SKI?
OH! THAT'S NO BUMP! IT'S DEEDEE!

EAT MY WAKE, GEORGINA!
HEY!

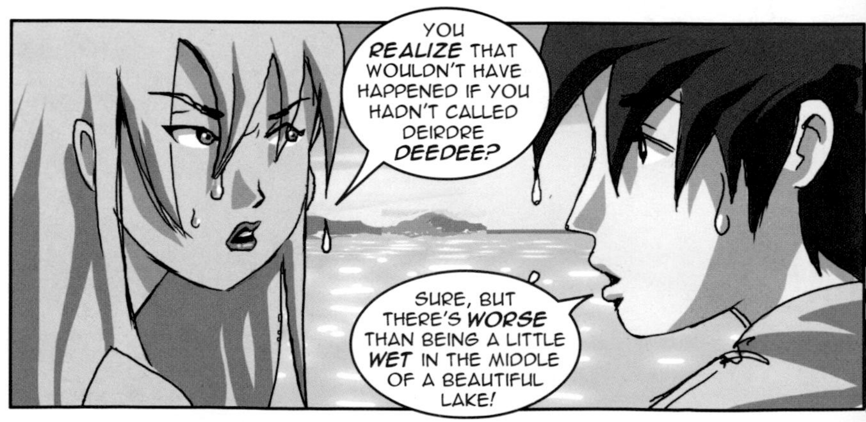
YOU REALIZE THAT WOULDN'T HAVE HAPPENED IF YOU HADN'T CALLED DEIRDRE DEEDEE?
SURE, BUT THERE'S WORSE THAN BEING A LITTLE WET IN THE MIDDLE OF A BEAUTIFUL LAKE!

ONLY NOW YOU'LL HAVE TO SPEND THE DAY FIGURING OUT HOW TO GET HER *BACK* FOR CALLING YOU *GEORGINA*.
YEAH, WELL. IT'S A HOBBY.
UMM... DOES THE LAKE WATER SEEM *STRANGE* TO YOU GUYS?
ONLY BECAUSE DEEDEE'S IN IT.
REALLY, NANCY, YOUR BRAIN IS WORKING OVERTIME!
WHAT COULD POSSIBLY BE WRONG ON SUCH A *BEAUTI-FUL*...

I KNOW YOU'RE NOT GOING TO BELIEVE THIS, BUT SOMETIMES LAKES CAN JUST VANISH!
YIKES!
HOW, YOU MAY ASK? A SINKHOLE! THAT'S A NATURAL DEPRESSION THAT FORMS IN THE LAND AND CONNECTS TO AN UNDERGROUND PASSAGE OR A CAVERN.
SOMETIMES THEY FORM SUDDENLY AND SWALLOW WHOLE HOUSES!
SO, ONCE IN A GREAT WHILE, IF A BIG SINKHOLE OPENS BELOW A LAKE, ALL THE WATER GOES IN!
IN 2004 IN WILDWOOD MISSOURI, A 23 ACRE LAKE COMPLETELY DRAINED AWAY!
THAT TOOK TWO DAYS.
HOLD ON!
THIS SEEMED TO BE HAPPENING A LOT FASTER!

ASIDE FROM WHAT'D HAPPEN IF WE WENT DOWN THE SINKHOLE, THE BIG PROBLEM WOULD BE IF THE BOAT CAPSIZED!
CAPSIZING IS WHEN THE MAIN MAST GOES EVEN WITH THE WATER. WHEN THE MAST GOES UNDER WATER, IT'S CALLED TURTLING.
I DON'T KNOW WHAT YOU CALL IT WHEN THE SAILBOAT ALMOST TIPS OVER BECAUSE THE LAKE IS VANISHING. I BET EVEN THE BEST SAILORS HAVEN'T INVENTED A WORD FOR THAT ONE.
I DID KNOW THE BOAT COULD EASILY CRUSH US, IF IT LANDED ON US UPSIDE DOWN!
MOST CAPSIZING OCCURS WHEN YOU TRY TO GIBE, OR SWING THE MAINSAIL FROM ONE SIDE TO THE OTHER.
THE MOST EFFECTIVE WAY TO AVOID THIS IS TO LET GO OF THE MAIN SAIL AND LET THE WIND TAKE IT WHERE IT WANTS.
THEN GET THE HECK OUT OF ITS WAY!

THE LAKE LOOKED LIKE A GIANT **BATHTUB** WITH THE DRAIN OPEN. ALL AROUND US, BOATS, SKIERS, FISHERMAN AND SWIMMERS WERE SWIRLING DOWN TO THE BOTTOM!

IF WE WEREN'T SO ***PANICKED***, WE MIGHT HAVE REALLY APPRECIATED WHAT A ***RARE*** EVENT WE WERE WITNESSING!

AS IT WAS, I HELD ON, WHILE BESS AND GEORGE ***SCREAMED***.

FORTUNATELY, WE MISSED THE SINKHOLE BY TEN YARDS, AND THE BOAT CAME DOWN ON THE LAKE BOTTOM!
THOK

EVERYONE *OKAY*?
DEFINE "OKAY."
I'LL NEVER LOOK AT A *TOILET* THE SAME WAY AGAIN.

WE WERE A LITTLE BRUISED AND *VERY* SHAKEN. IT LOOKED LIKE EVERYONE *ELSE* ON THE LAKE WAS, TOO.
HELP!
SOME-ONE HELP! I THINK I'M GOING TO...

IT WAS HARD TO FEEL BAD FOR HER. BUT RIGHT THEN I DID.
WOK
NANCY DREW, YOU KNEW THE LAKE WAS GOING TO VANISH, DIDN'T YOU? AND YOU DIDN'T WARN ME JUST SO I WOULD RUIN MY JET SKI!
THEN SHE OPENED HER MOUTH AND I DIDN'T FEEL BAD FOR HER AT ALL.
I STILL DIDN'T HAVE THE HEART TO TELL HER THAT HER FATHER'S NEW LAKE-SIDE CABIN HAD JUST GONE DOWN IN VALUE.
WHAT WITHOUT IT HAVING THE LAKE AND ALL.
THE BOTTOM'S PRETTY MUDDY, BUT I THINK IT CAN HOLD US. BRACE YOURSELF. IT FEELS GROSS.
YUCK!

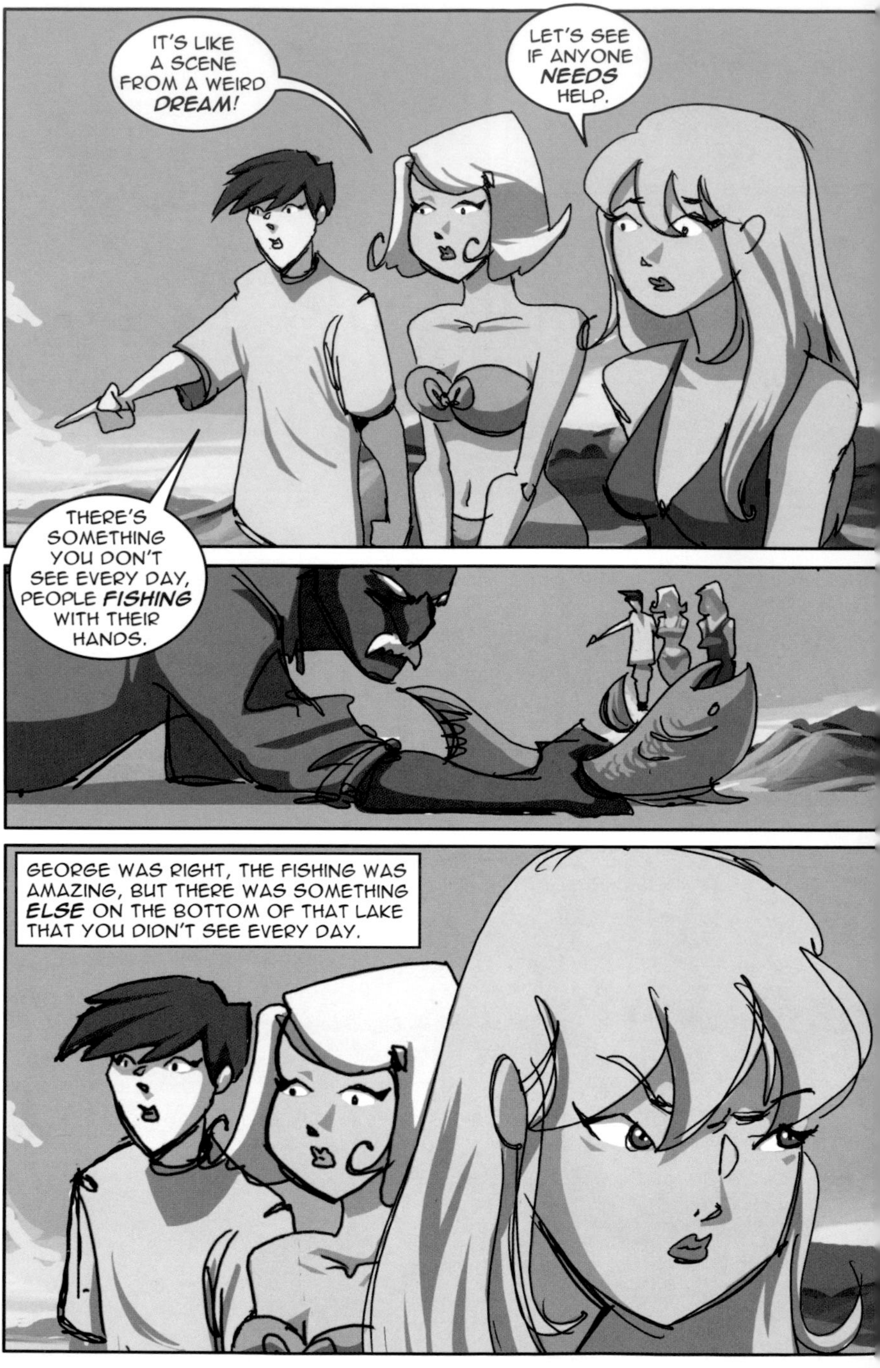

IT'S LIKE A SCENE FROM A WEIRD *DREAM*!
LET'S SEE IF ANYONE *NEEDS* HELP.
THERE'S SOMETHING YOU DON'T SEE EVERY DAY, PEOPLE *FISHING* WITH THEIR HANDS.

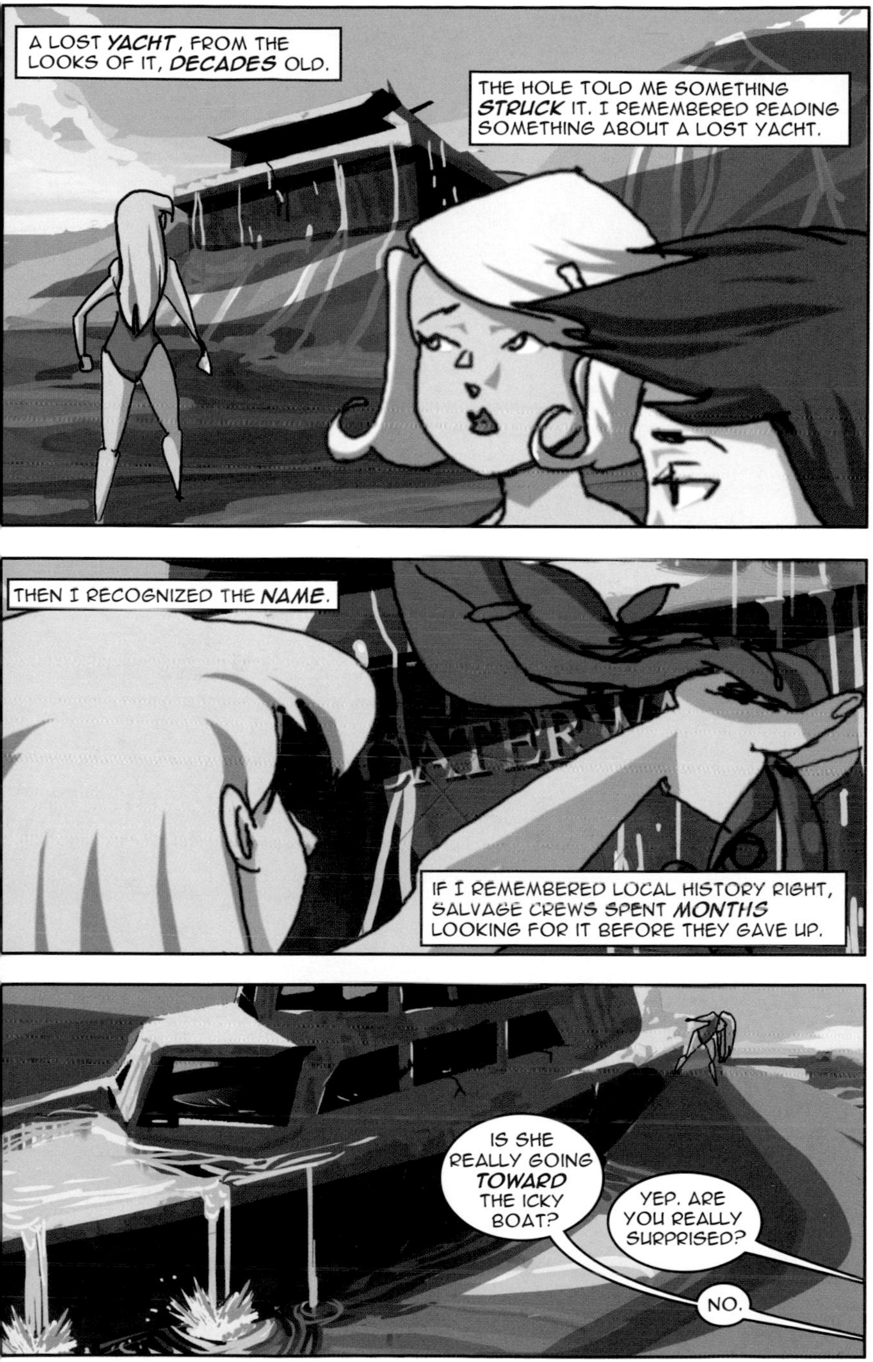

A LOST *YACHT*, FROM THE LOOKS OF IT, *DECADES* OLD.

THE HOLE TOLD ME SOMETHING *STRUCK* IT. I REMEMBERED READING SOMETHING ABOUT A LOST YACHT.

EASY, NANCY! THAT WOOD'S BEEN WATER-SOAKED FOR YEARS! IT COULD JUST FALL APART.
SHE WAS RIGHT, OF COURSE, BUT SOMETIMES I GET SO CURIOUS, I JUST FORGET WHAT I'M DOING.
BESIDES, I FIGURED WHAT HARM COULD THERE BE IN JUST GIVING A LITTLE TUG TO THE LADDER?
UH-OH.
CAROOOOFF!
A SECOND LATER, I HAD MY ANSWER.
A WHOLE LOT OF HARM. THE ENTIRE SIDE OF THE BOAT CAME OFF!
WOOMF!

WOW! WITH THE WALL DOWN, YOU CAN SEE EVERY-THING!
CHECK IT OUT! THE BEDS ARE STILL MADE.
THERE ARE PLATES ON THE TABLE! AND LOOK AT THAT OLD BOOM BOX!
MY BRAIN DANCED BETWEEN WHAT I SAW AND WHAT I WAS TRYING TO REMEMBER.
IT ALL CAME TOGETHER WHEN MY EYES WENT STRAIGHT TOWARD...
A SAFE!
THAT'S WHY THE SALVAGE CREWS SPENT SO MUCH TIME LOOKING FOR THIS SHIP!
YOU MEAN, WE FOUND LIKE A SUNKEN TREASURE? LET'S LOOK INSIDE!
THERE'S NO WAY WE CAN OPEN IT HERE. YOU'D NEED A BLOWTORCH OR A SAFE-CRACKER!

OH, I THINK I CAN HANDLE THIS, GIRLS.

REALLY? HAVE YOU BEEN STUDYING SAFE-CRACKING?

NOT EXACTLY.

I JUST NOTICED THAT THE **HINGES** SEEM RUSTED THROUGH!

WHICH MEANS, I SHOULD BE ABLE TO PULL THE DOOR...

OFF?

HEY-HEY-HEY! I'M BUYIN' A NEW PDA AND A NEW **CAR** TO DRIVE IT AROUND IN!

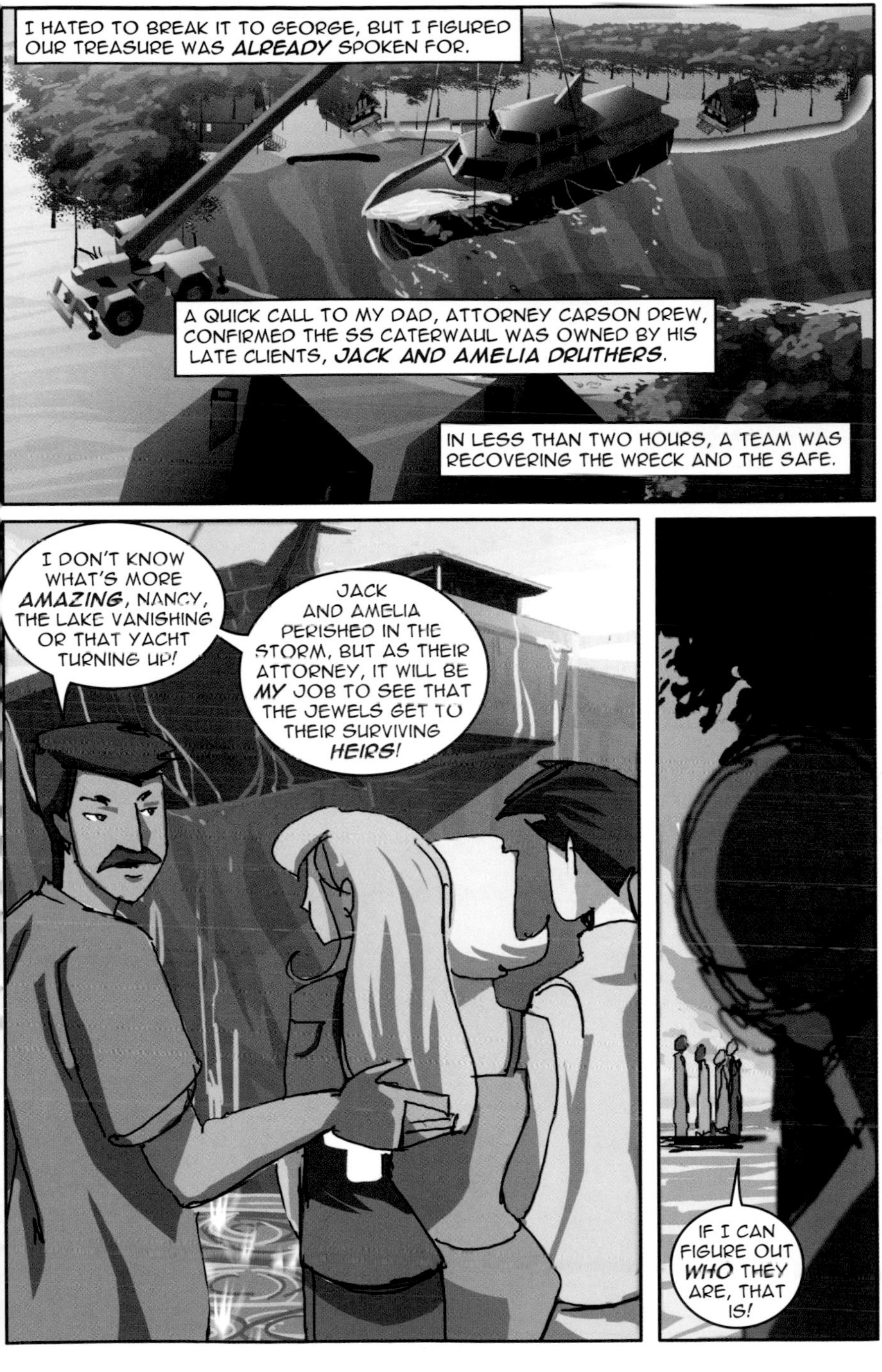

I HATED TO BREAK IT TO GEORGE, BUT I FIGURED OUR TREASURE WAS *ALREADY* SPOKEN FOR.

A QUICK CALL TO MY DAD, ATTORNEY CARSON DREW, CONFIRMED THE SS CATERWAUL WAS OWNED BY HIS LATE CLIENTS, *JACK AND AMELIA DRUTHERS*.

IN LESS THAN TWO HOURS, A TEAM WAS RECOVERING THE WRECK AND THE SAFE.

I DON'T KNOW WHAT'S MORE *AMAZING*, NANCY, THE LAKE VANISHING OR THAT YACHT TURNING UP!

JACK AND AMELIA PERISHED IN THE STORM, BUT AS THEIR ATTORNEY, IT WILL BE *MY* JOB TO SEE THAT THE JEWELS GET TO THEIR SURVIVING *HEIRS*!

WHILE DAD DID HIS LAWYER THING, WE SPENT THE LATE AFTERNOON AT THE RIVER HEIGHTS PEDIATRIC HOSPITAL AS VOLUNTEERS FOR PROJECT SUNSHINE.
project sunshine
ONCE A MONTH, WE DO A LITTLE ACT FOR ALL THE CHILDREN WITH SERIOUS ILLNESSES, JUST TO TRY TO BRING THEM, WELL, A LITTLE SUNSHINE.
CAN YOU MAKE A BALLOON THAT LOOKS LIKE A DRAINING LAKE?
UH...
TODAY, THOUGH, ALL THEY WANTED TO HEAR ABOUT WAS THE LAKE!

WE DECIDED TO DRIVE TO THE DOCK TO TAKE ANOTHER LOOK AT THE ***YACHT***, NOW THAT IT'D BEEN PULLED ASHORE.

THANKS FOR THE ***HAT***, NANCE!

SO, ***GIVE***! WHAT'D YOUR DAD SAY ABOUT THE DRUTHERS?

WELL, IT'S YOUR TYPICAL GET RICH ***QUICK***, GET CRAZY AND GET POOR ***QUICKER***, STORY!

ACK!

"THE DRUTHERS MADE A FORTUNE SELLING FAX PAPER IN THE EARLY 1980s."

"THEY LIVED THE GOOD LIFE FOR YEARS, LIMOS, ESTATES, TWO AIRPLANES."

"BUT THEIR FAVORITE PLACE WAS THEIR YACHT, THE ***CATERWAUL***. THEY WERE ON IT NEARLY EVERY DAY, MOVING IT FROM LAKE TO LAKE."

YOU'D THINK ALL THAT MONEY MIGHT MAKE THEM HAPPY, BUT AMELIA DRUTHERS WAS *MISERABLE*!
SHE SPENT ALL HER TIME BEING *TERRIFIED* THAT SHE MIGHT LOSE HER MONEY AND BECOME POOR AGAIN.
SHE'D EVEN KEEP HER JEWELS WITH HER WHEREVER THEY WENT, LIKE A SECURITY BLANKET.
HENCE THE *SAFE* ON THEIR YACHT?
YEP!
IT SEEMED LIKE A SAFE PLACE. THEY WERE ALWAYS ON IT, IN ALL KINDS OF WEATHER, RAIN OR SHINE.
AND THEN, WELL, THE SHINING STOPPED AND IT *REALLY* RAINED!
"WITNESSES SAY A FREAK STORM SLAMMED THE CATERWAUL INTO A ROCKY PART OF THE LAKESHORE AND IT SANK THE BOAT, ALONG WITH AMELIA AND JACK DRUTHERS!"
POP

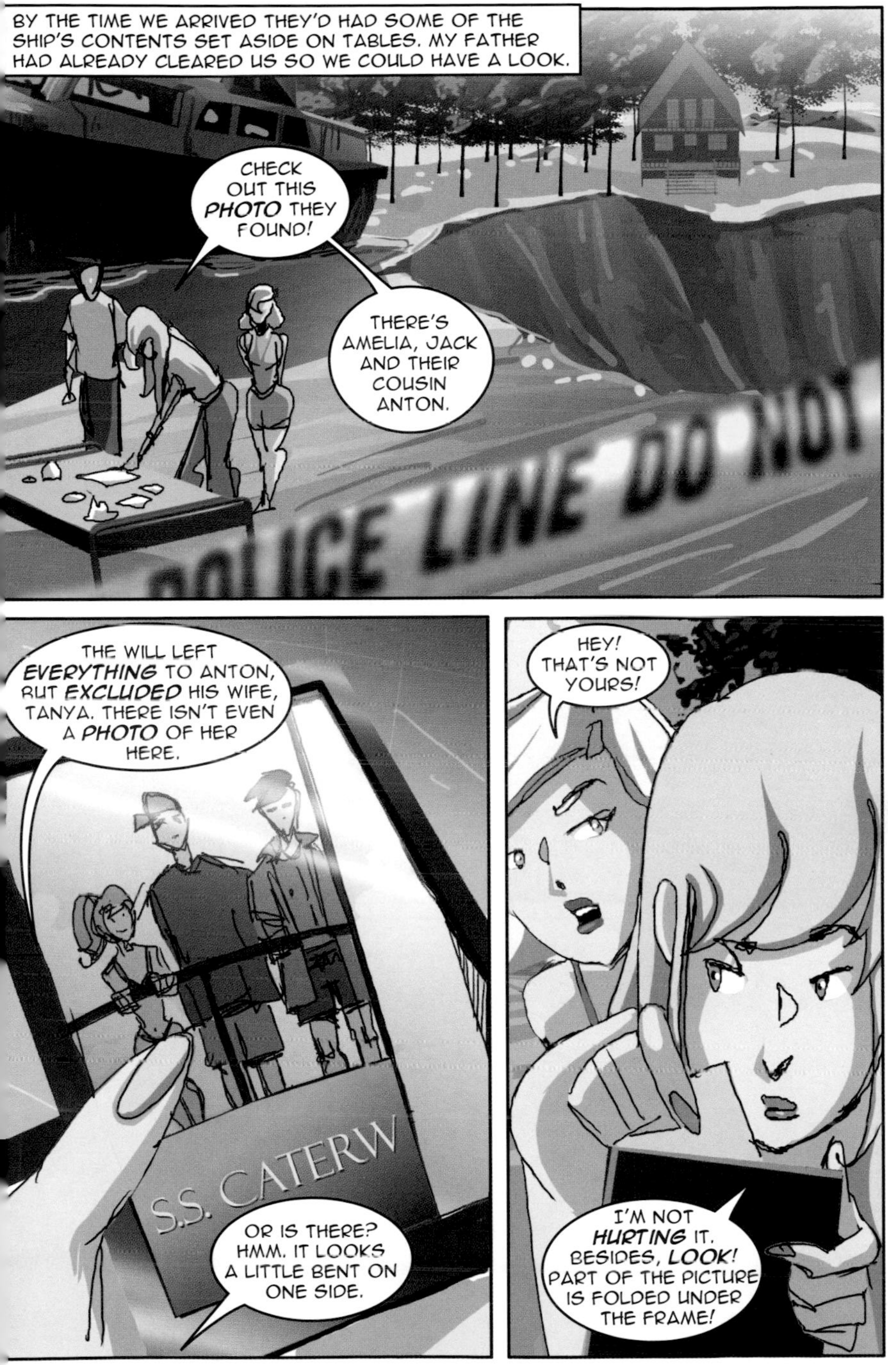

BY THE TIME WE ARRIVED THEY'D HAD SOME OF THE SHIP'S CONTENTS SET ASIDE ON TABLES. MY FATHER HAD ALREADY CLEARED US SO WE COULD HAVE A LOOK.

CHECK OUT THIS *PHOTO* THEY FOUND!

THERE'S AMELIA, JACK AND THEIR COUSIN ANTON.

POLICE LINE DO NOT

THIS USED TO BE A PICTURE OF TANYA, TOO, BUT SOME-ONE CROSSED HER OUT. PROBABLY AMELIA.
WHY'D SHE HATE HER SO MUCH?
SHE THOUGHT EVERYONE WAS AFTER HER MONEY. THAT'S PROBABLY WHY SHE KEPT TANYA OUT OF THE WILL.
ANYWAY, ANTON AND TANYA SPENT THE INHERITANCE AND DROVE THE BUSINESS INTO BANKRUPTCY.
NO HAPPY ENDING HERE, EH?
GETS WORSE. TANYA DRUTHERS STILL COMES TO TOWN ON RARE OCCASIONS, BUT NO ONE'S SEEN ANTON DRUTHERS IN TEN YEARS!
THERE ARE RUMORS SHE MURDERED HIM!

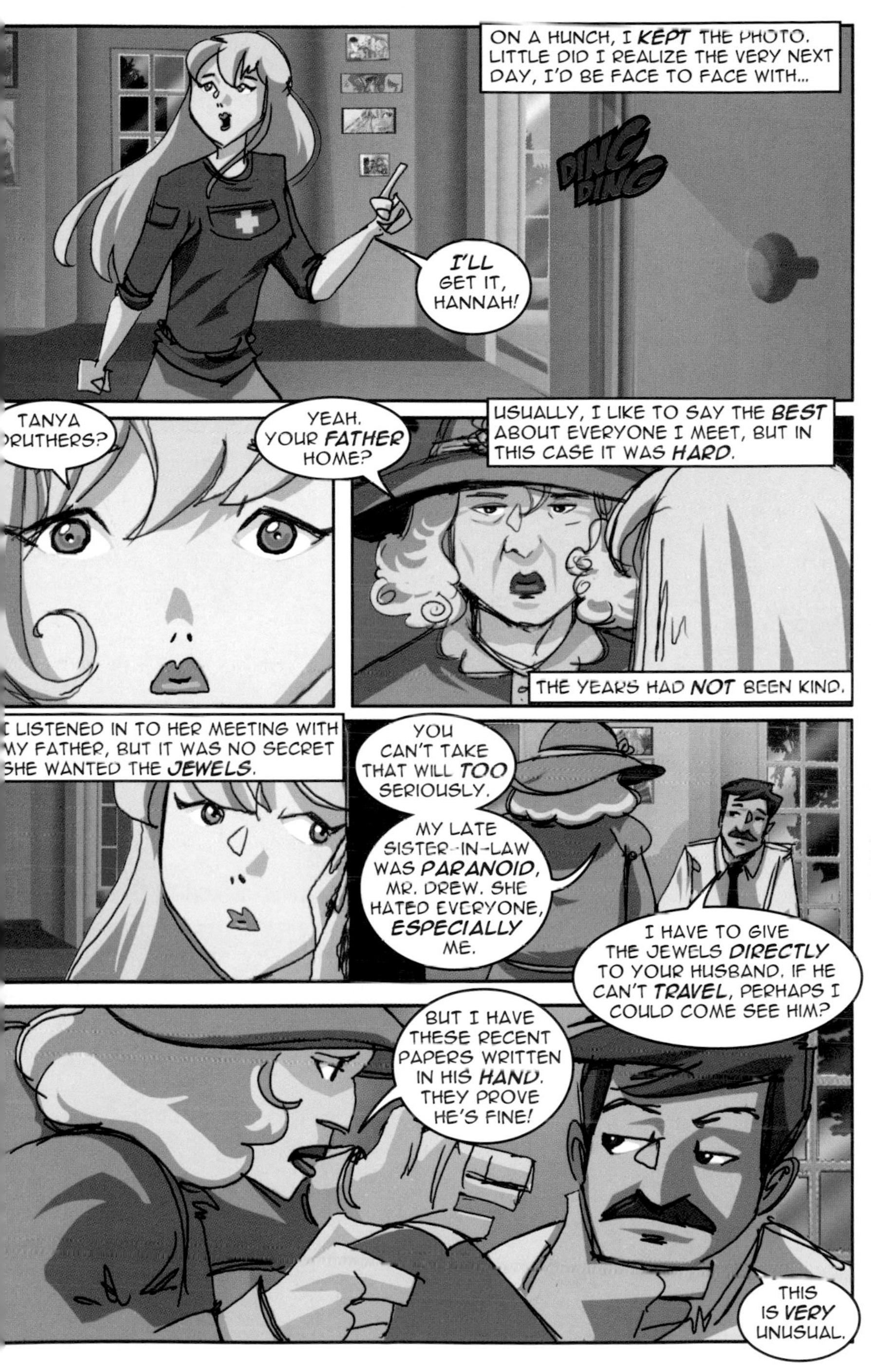
ON A HUNCH, I KEPT THE PHOTO. LITTLE DID I REALIZE THE VERY NEXT DAY, I'D BE FACE TO FACE WITH...
DING DING
I'LL GET IT, HANNAH!
TANYA DRUTHERS?
YEAH. YOUR FATHER HOME?
USUALLY, I LIKE TO SAY THE BEST ABOUT EVERYONE I MEET, BUT IN THIS CASE IT WAS HARD.
THE YEARS HAD NOT BEEN KIND.
I LISTENED IN TO HER MEETING WITH MY FATHER, BUT IT WAS NO SECRET SHE WANTED THE JEWELS.
YOU CAN'T TAKE THAT WILL TOO SERIOUSLY.
MY LATE SISTER-IN-LAW WAS PARANOID, MR. DREW. SHE HATED EVERYONE, ESPECIALLY ME.
I HAVE TO GIVE THE JEWELS DIRECTLY TO YOUR HUSBAND. IF HE CAN'T TRAVEL, PERHAPS I COULD COME SEE HIM?
BUT I HAVE THESE RECENT PAPERS WRITTEN IN HIS HAND. THEY PROVE HE'S FINE!
THIS IS VERY UNUSUAL.

WELL, FOR STARTERS, PLEASE HAVE YOUR HUSBAND FILL OUT THESE FORMS SO I CAN GET THE PAPERWORK GOING.
BUT, I'M SORRY, MRS. DRUTHERS, WE ***WILL*** HAVE TO ARRANGE A ***MEETING***.

I FELT THE SAME WAY, BUT THAT ONLY MADE ME MORE CURIOUS. WHAT WAS SHE TRYING TO HIDE? HAD SHE KILLED ANTON?
THE MUFFLER ON HER OLD CAR WAS FULL OF HOLES, WHICH MADE IT EASY TO FOLLOW.
SHE DROVE OUT OF TOWN, PAST SOME FIELDS, INTO THE WOODS.
THEN STOPPED IN THE MIDDLE OF NOWHERE!
NOW, USUALLY, MY HEAD GETS SO WRAPPED UP IN A MYSTERY I FORGET THINGS LIKE FILLING MY GAS TANK.
BESS AND GEORGE LIKE TO JOKE I'M THE ONLY PERSON IN THE WORLD WHO CAN RUN OUT OF GAS IN A HYBRID!
BUT THIS TIME, I'D TANKED UP YESTER-DAY, SO I WOULD NOT HAVE ANY TROUBLE MAKING A QUICK GETAWAY.

JUST AS WELL. THE OLD TRAILER MRS. DRUTHERS WALKED INTO LOOKED MORE *CREEPY* THAN A HAUNTED HOUSE.

I GUESS THEY'D BEEN FORCED TO LIVE *HERE* AFTER THEY LOST ALL THEIR MONEY!

ONCE THEY'D HAD IT *ALL*, NOW NOTHING. LIKE DEIRDRE, THOUGH, IT WAS HARD TO FEEL *TOO* BAD FOR THEM, SINCE THEY'D DONE IT TO THEMSELVES.

I WAS HOPING TO SEE MR. DRUTHERS, BUT I *DIDN'T*.

INSTEAD, MRS. DRUTHERS PUT THE DOCUMENTS ON A TABLE, FOUND HERSELF A *PEN*...

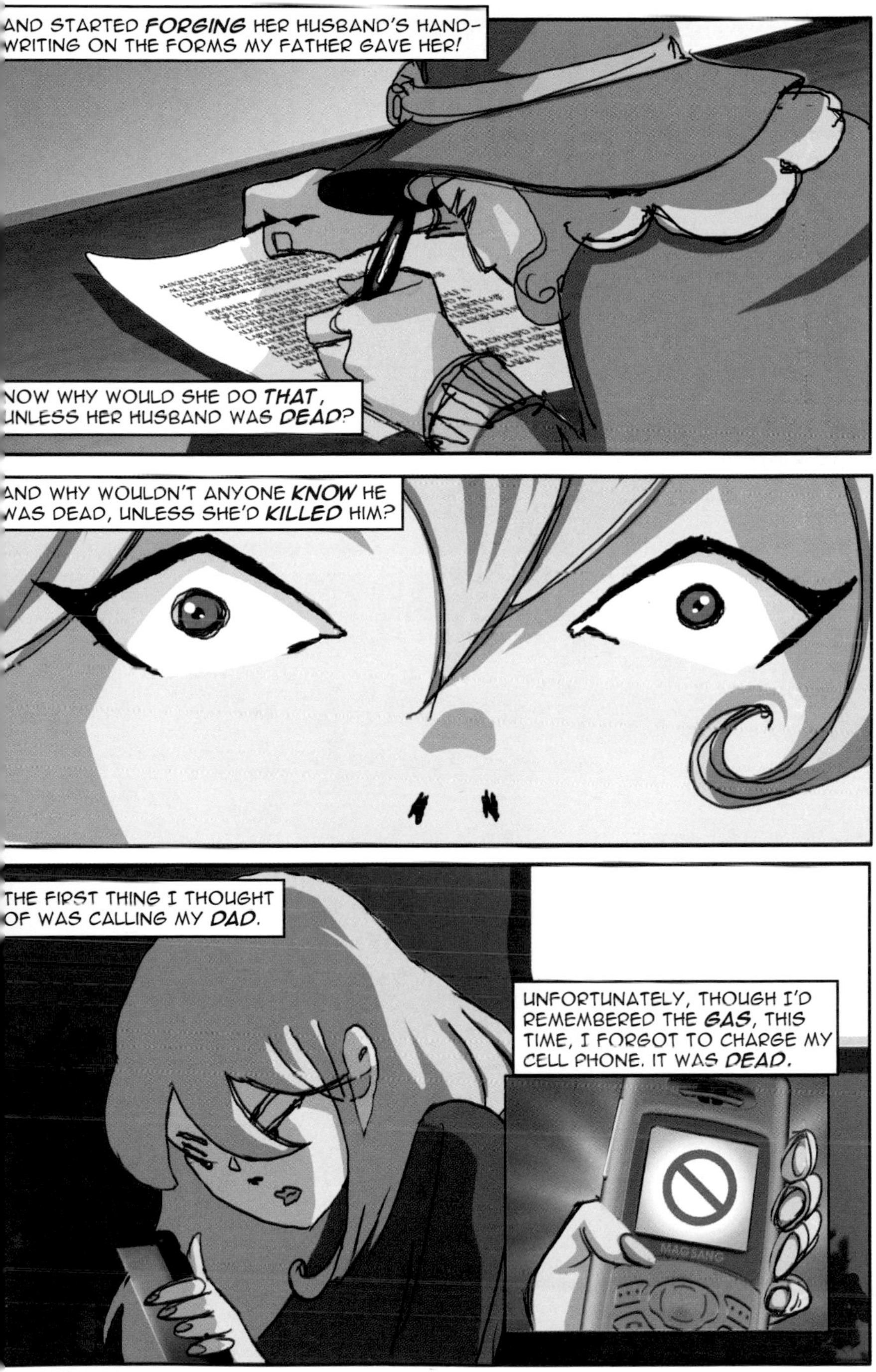

AND STARTED *FORGING* HER HUSBAND'S HAND-WRITING ON THE FORMS MY FATHER GAVE HER!

NOW WHY WOULD SHE DO *THAT*, UNLESS HER HUSBAND WAS *DEAD*?

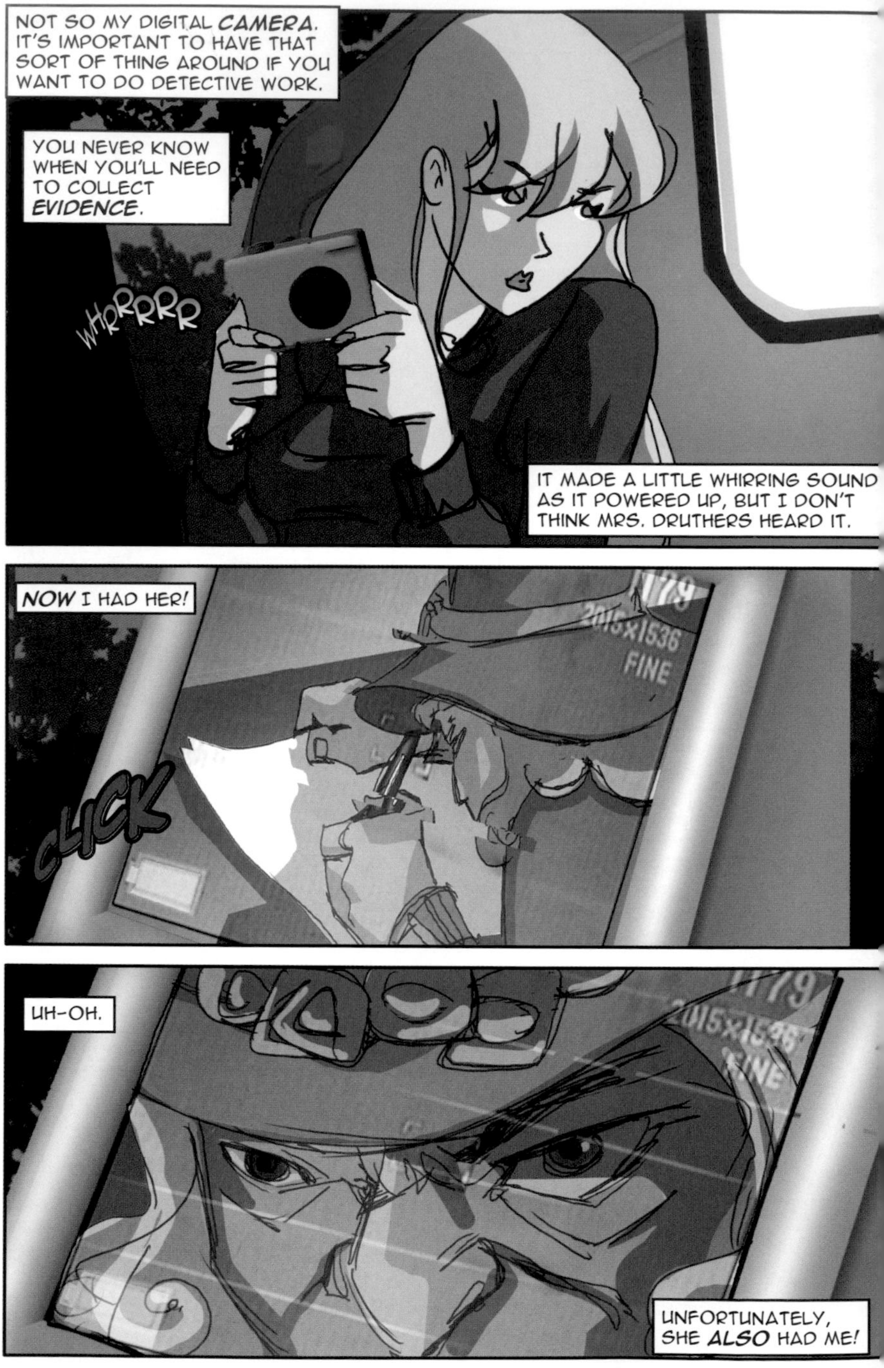

NOT SO MY DIGITAL **CAMERA**. IT'S IMPORTANT TO HAVE THAT SORT OF THING AROUND IF YOU WANT TO DO DETECTIVE WORK.

YOU NEVER KNOW WHEN YOU'LL NEED TO COLLECT ***EVIDENCE***.

WHRRRRR

IT MADE A LITTLE WHIRRING SOUND AS IT POWERED UP, BUT I DON'T THINK MRS. DRUTHERS HEARD IT.

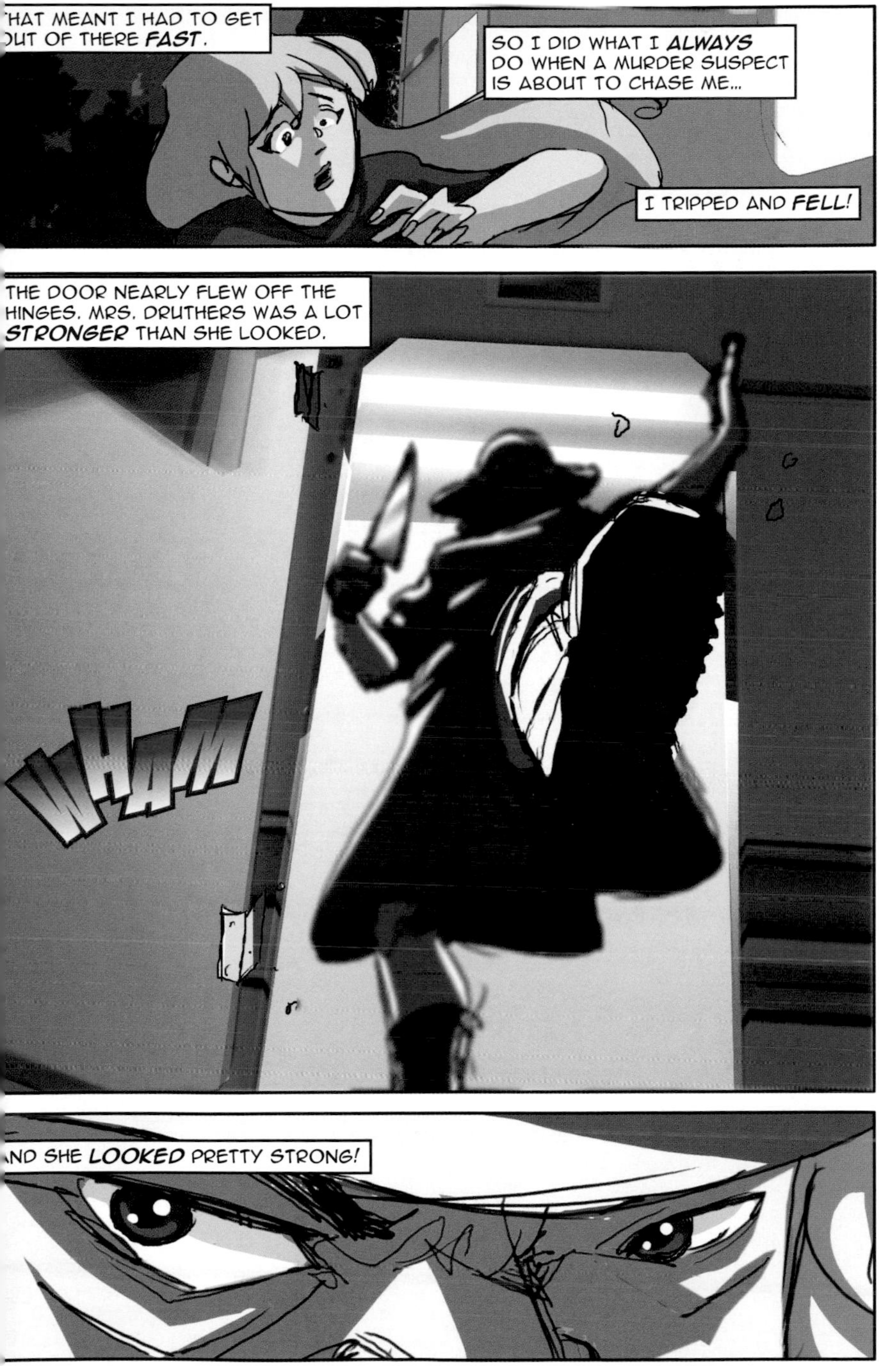

THE DOOR NEARLY FLEW OFF THE HINGES. MRS. DRUTHERS WAS A LOT *STRONGER* THAN SHE LOOKED.

WHAM

BEFORE SHE COULD SPOT ME, I MANAGED TO HIDE.
BRANCHES SCRATCHED MY ARMS, BUT I BIT MY TONGUE TO KEEP FROM CRYING OUT.
AFTER ALL, MRS. DRUTHERS WAS RIGHT ABOVE ME! I COULD HEAR HER SLOW, PUFFING BREATHS.
AND I WAS TERRIFIED I'D FIND HER HUSBAND THE HARD WAY!
END CHAPTER ONE

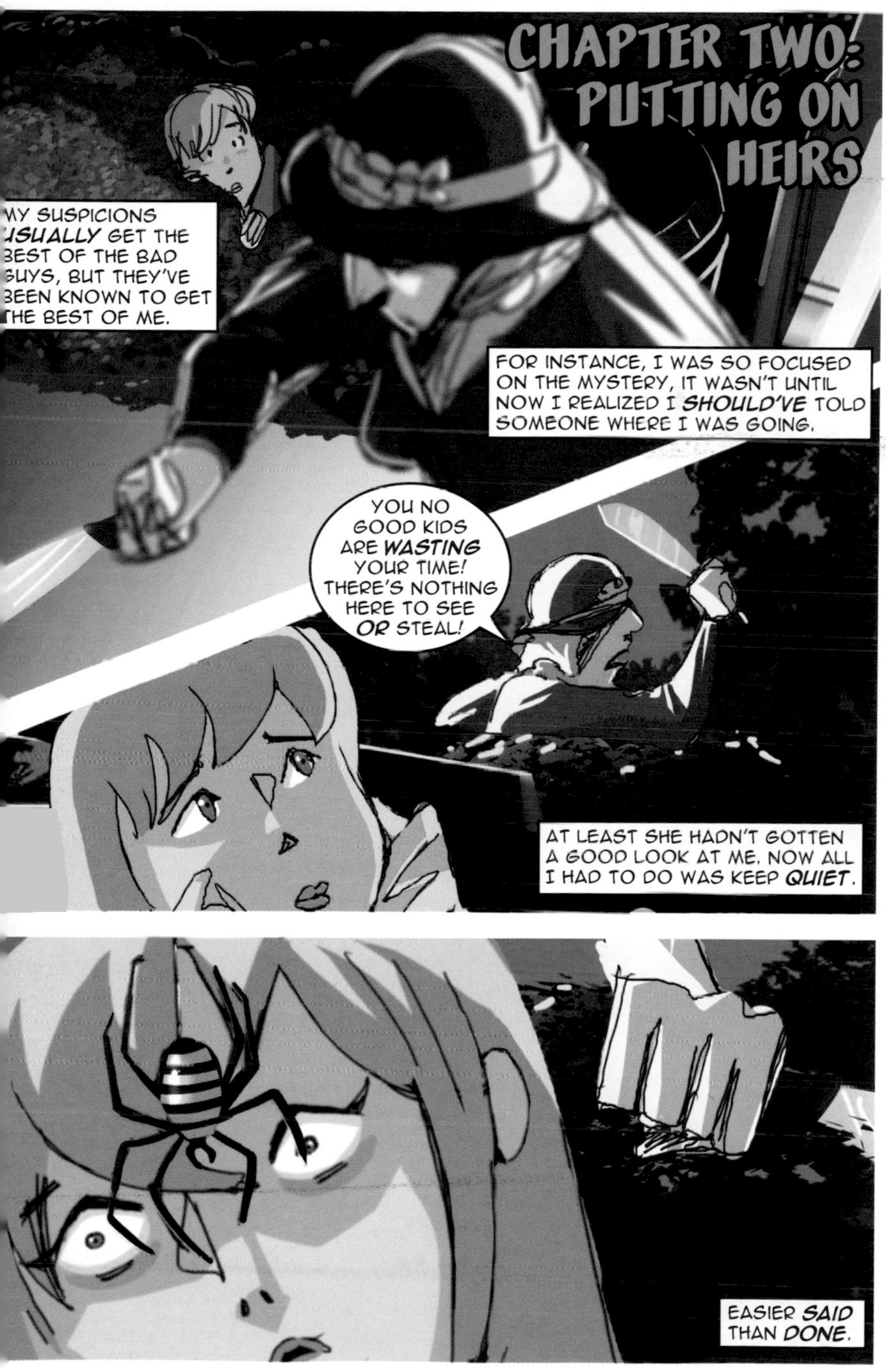

CHAPTER TWO: PUTTING ON HEIRS

MY SUSPICIONS *USUALLY* GET THE BEST OF THE BAD GUYS, BUT THEY'VE BEEN KNOWN TO GET THE BEST OF ME.

FOR INSTANCE, I WAS SO FOCUSED ON THE MYSTERY, IT WASN'T UNTIL NOW I REALIZED I *SHOULD'VE* TOLD SOMEONE WHERE I WAS GOING.

YOU NO GOOD KIDS ARE *WASTING* YOUR TIME! THERE'S NOTHING HERE TO SEE *OR* STEAL!

AT LEAST SHE HADN'T GOTTEN A GOOD LOOK AT ME. NOW ALL I HAD TO DO WAS KEEP *QUIET*.

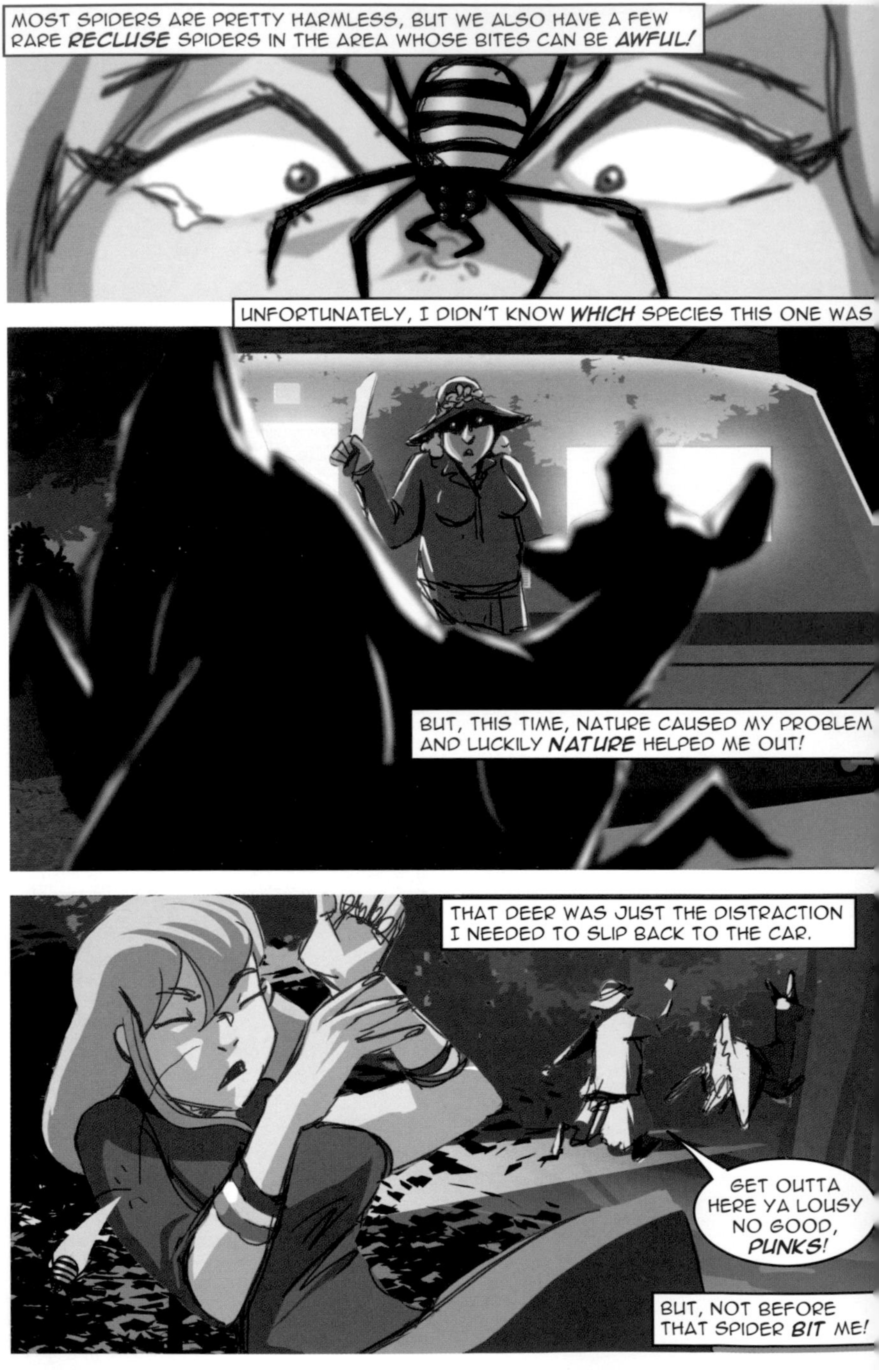

MOST SPIDERS ARE PRETTY HARMLESS, BUT WE ALSO HAVE A FEW RARE ***RECLUSE*** SPIDERS IN THE AREA WHOSE BITES CAN BE ***AWFUL!***

UNFORTUNATELY, I DIDN'T KNOW ***WHICH*** SPECIES THIS ONE WAS

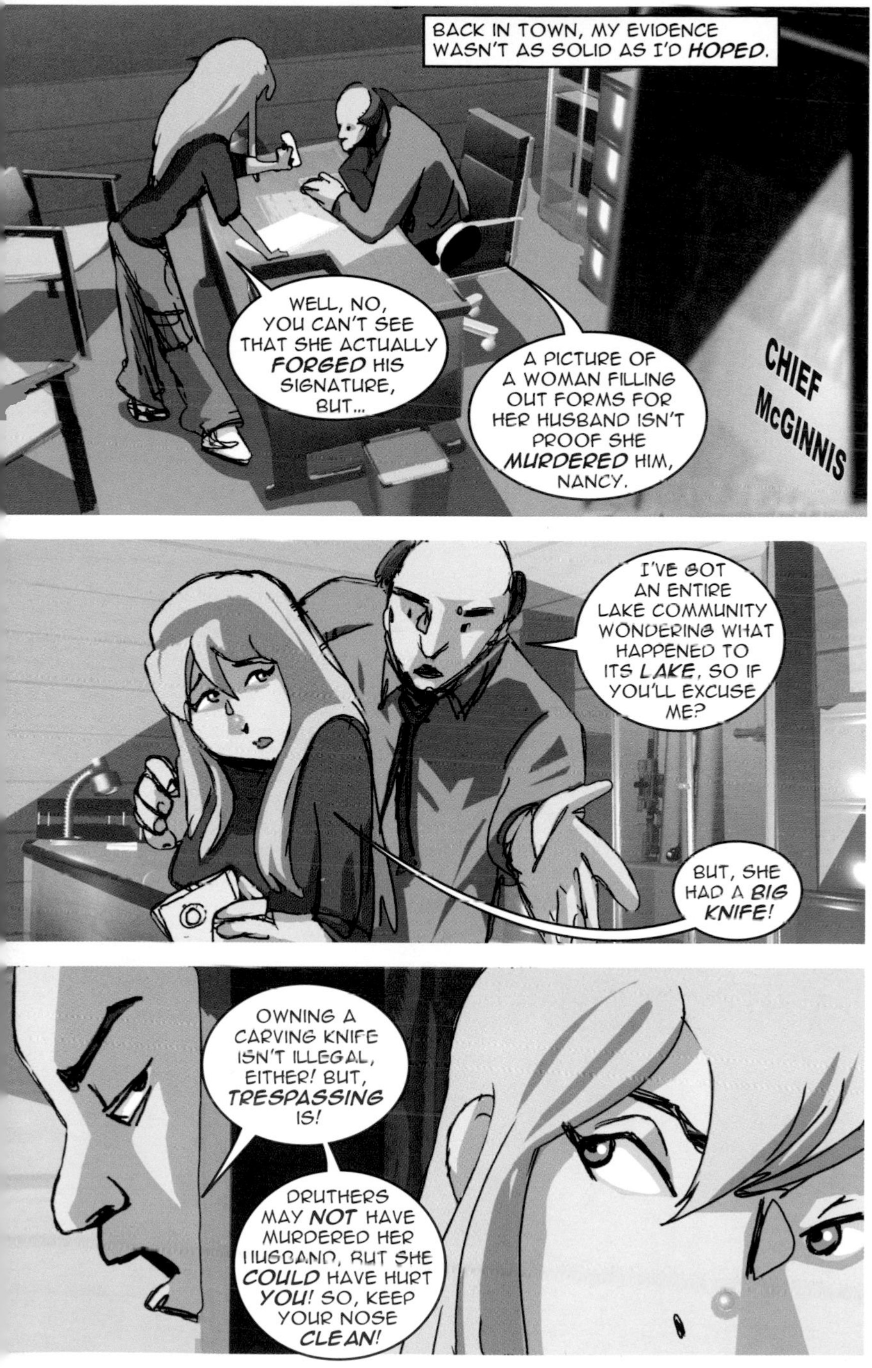

BACK IN TOWN, MY EVIDENCE WASN'T AS SOLID AS I'D ***HOPED.***

WELL, NO, YOU CAN'T SEE THAT SHE ACTUALLY ***FORGED*** HIS SIGNATURE, BUT...

A PICTURE OF A WOMAN FILLING OUT FORMS FOR HER HUSBAND ISN'T PROOF SHE ***MURDERED*** HIM, NANCY.

CHIEF McGINNIS

HEY, NANCE! WHAT'S UP WITH THE STAND UP? YOU WERE SUPPOSED TO MEET US FOR LUNCH!
SORRY! GOT A LITTLE DISTRACTED WITH A MYSTERY!
TOLD YOU!
R.H.P
DON'T SWEAT IT, NANCY. WE ATE A SECOND DESERT IN YOUR HONOR.
BUT IT LOOKS LIKE YOU GOT THE ZIT! WANT ME TO POP IT?!
UM, EWW!
WHAT?! FRIENDS DON'T LET FRIENDS WALK AROUND WITH NOSE-PIMPLES!
IT'S NOT A PIMPLE! A SPIDER BIT ME WHEN I WAS HIDING FROM A KILLER WITH A BUTCHER KNIFE!

NATURALLY!
I'VE GOT TO CALL MY DAD TO SEE IF HE GOT THOSE SIGNED FORMS BACK YET. MRS. DRUTHERS MAY ACTUALLY DELIVER THE EVIDENCE OF HER GUILT!
OR NOT. SIGH.
BATTERY'S DEAD.
HERE. IT'S MY SPARE. JUST DON'T MAKE ANY TWENTY MINUTE CALLS TO DELHI!
THANKS!

AFTER I EXPLAINED WHAT HAPPENED, DAD CALLED ON *HANDWRITING* EXPERT BILL DALE.
ALL MR. DALE HAD TO DO WAS *CONFIRM* THAT THE HANDWRITING ON THAT FORM DID *NOT* BELONG TO MR. DRUTHERS! IT WAS A SLAM DUNK!

BUT, AS I SHOULD KNOW BY NOW, THERE ARE *NO* SLAM DUNKS IN DETECTIVE WORK!
NO DOUBT ABOUT IT... THESE TWO DOCUMENTS WERE *DEFINITELY* WRITTEN BY THE *SAME* HAND.

THAT'S IMPOSSIBLE! I SAW *MRS*. DRUTHERS FILLING OUT *THAT* FORM. AND MY FATHER SAW *MR.* DRUTHERS SIGN THE *OTHER* TEN YEARS AGO!
NOT TO BOAST, BUT I'M PRETTY *GOOD* AT SPOTTING FORGERIES!

I GUESS I'M **STUMPED** ON THIS ONE.
YOU? STUMPED?

SOMETIMES HE ANSWER IS ON THE *TIP* OF YOUR NOSE!
OWW! NOT FUNNY.

SORRY. IS THAT, A *PIMPLE*?!
UH, A *SPIDER-BITE*.
I DOUBTED DAD WOULD *ENJOY* THE STORY OF MY HIDING IN THE BUSH, SO I LEFT *OUT* THE DETAILS.

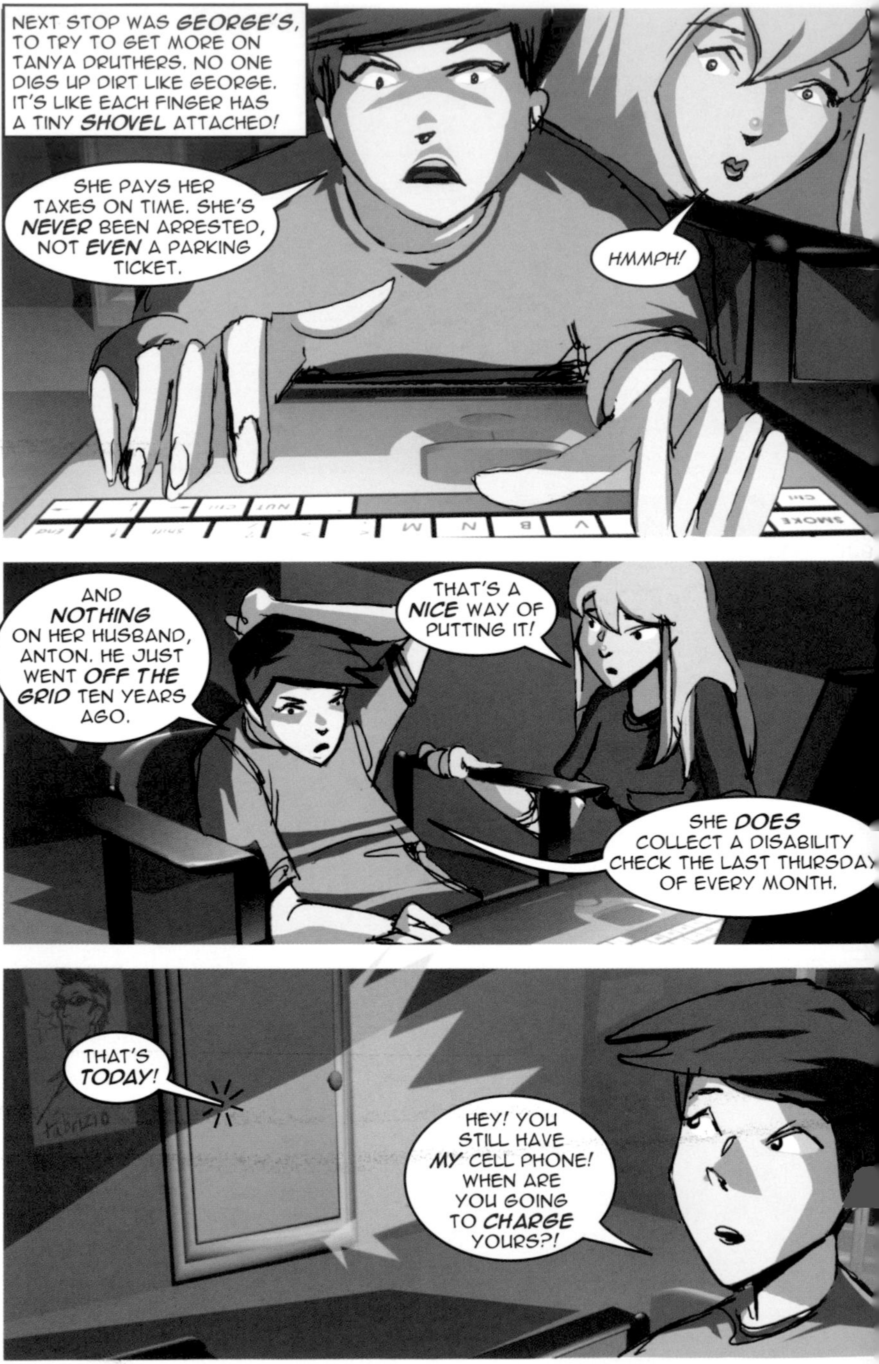

NEXT STOP WAS *GEORGE'S*, TO TRY TO GET MORE ON TANYA DRUTHERS. NO ONE DIGS UP DIRT LIKE GEORGE. IT'S LIKE EACH FINGER HAS A TINY *SHOVEL* ATTACHED!

SHE PAYS HER TAXES ON TIME. SHE'S *NEVER* BEEN ARRESTED, NOT *EVEN* A PARKING TICKET.

HMMPH!

AND *NOTHING* ON HER HUSBAND, ANTON. HE JUST WENT *OFF THE GRID* TEN YEARS AGO.

THAT'S A *NICE* WAY OF PUTTING IT!

SHE *DOES* COLLECT A DISABILITY CHECK THE LAST THURSDAY OF EVERY MONTH.

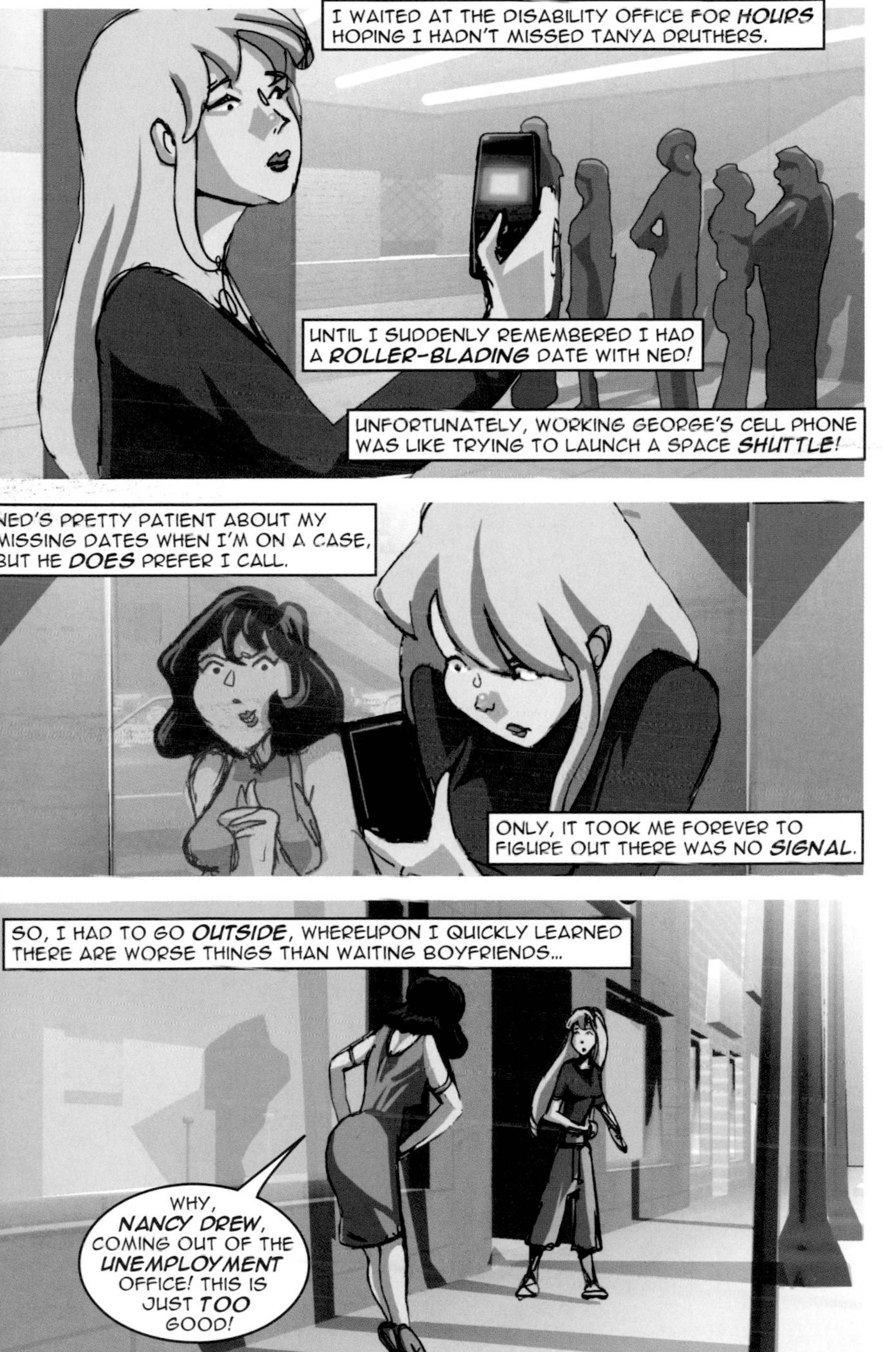
I WAITED AT THE DISABILITY OFFICE FOR HOURS HOPING I HADN'T MISSED TANYA DRUTHERS.
UNTIL I SUDDENLY REMEMBERED I HAD A ROLLER-BLADING DATE WITH NED!
UNFORTUNATELY, WORKING GEORGE'S CELL PHONE WAS LIKE TRYING TO LAUNCH A SPACE SHUTTLE!
NED'S PRETTY PATIENT ABOUT MY MISSING DATES WHEN I'M ON A CASE, BUT HE DOES PREFER I CALL.
ONLY, IT TOOK ME FOREVER TO FIGURE OUT THERE WAS NO SIGNAL.
SO, I HAD TO GO OUTSIDE, WHEREUPON I QUICKLY LEARNED THERE ARE WORSE THINGS THAN WAITING BOYFRIENDS...
WHY, NANCY DREW, COMING OUT OF THE UNEMPLOYMENT OFFICE! THIS IS JUST TOO GOOD!

I HEARD POOR PEOPLE HAVE LOUSY DIETS, BUT JUDGING BY THE SIZE OF THAT ZIT IT'S WORSE THAN I THOUGHT!
SIGH. HELLO, DIERDRE...
DON'T TELL ME YOUR FATHER'S LAW PRACTICE IS DOING SO BADLY YOU'RE ON WELFARE?!
ON SECOND THOUGHT, DO TELL ME THAT! PLEASE?
ANYONE EVER TELL YOU IT'S NOT NICE TO MOCK THE POOR?
HA! I THOUGHT YOU DIDN'T CARE ABOUT YOUR APPEARANCE, BUT IT SEEMS I STRUCK A NERVE.
UH-OH. FUN AS IT IS DISCUSSING MY SPIDER-BITE, GOTTA RUN!

I DIDN'T BOTHER TELLING DEIRDRE SHE *ALWAYS* STRIKES A NERVE, *LOTS* OF NERVES.
MEANWHILE, MRS. DRUTHERS HADN'T SEEN ME.
I WASN'T SURE SHE'D PAID MUCH ATTENTION TO ME WHEN WE MET, BUT, IF SHE *DID* RECOGNIZE ME, SHE'D BE *SUSPICIOUS*.
I WASN'T EVEN SURE WHAT I WAS HOPING TO *DISCOVER* BY FOLLOWING HER.
DID I REALLY THINK SHE'D LEAD ME TO HER MURDERED HUSBAND, THE *CORPUS DELICTI*?
THAT'S LATIN FOR "BODY OF THE CRIME," BY THE WAY.

NO SUCH LUCK.
SHE JUST WENT TO THE BANK.
TO DEPOSIT HER CHECK, I FIGURED.

OR AT LEAST THAT'S WHAT I THOUGHT. BUT, THEN SHE TOOK OUT A SAFE-DEPOSIT BOX.
IF SHE WAS AS POOR AS SHE SAID, WHAT WAS SHE KEEPING IN A SAFE-DEPOSIT BOX?

I WAS DYING TO SEE WHAT WAS INSIDE THAT BOX, BUT ALL I COULD DO WAS ACT NONCHALANT AND HOPE THIS WASN'T A BIG WASTE OF TIME.

THAT A PIMPLE, NANCY?
NO, MR. JENSEN. IT'S A SPIDER-BITE.
YOU SHOULD PUT SOME ANTIBIOTIC OINTMENT ON THAT, FOR SURE!

SO FAR TANYA DRUTHERS'S ERRANDS PROVIDED NO CLUES.
I HADN'T EXPECTED THEM TO. I JUST HOPED SHE WOULD GIVE ME SOMETHING, ANYTHING I COULD INVESTIGATE FURTHER...
...BEFORE I STARTED DIGGING UP THE WOODS AROUND HER TRAILER.

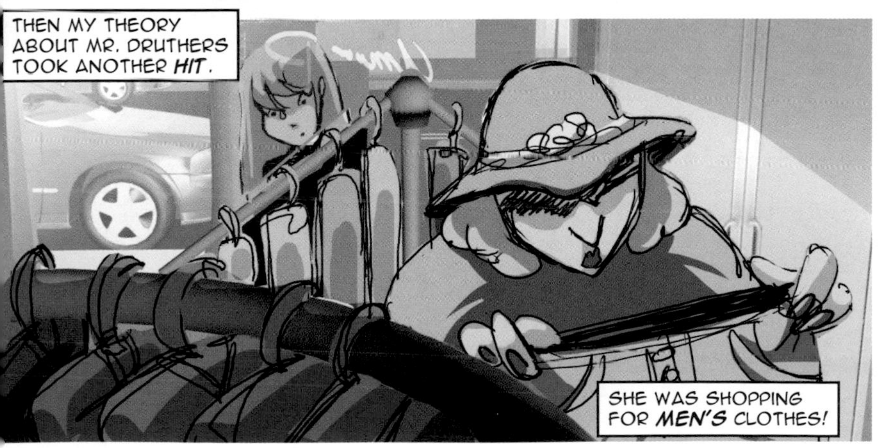
THEN MY THEORY ABOUT MR. DRUTHERS TOOK ANOTHER HIT.
SHE WAS SHOPPING FOR MEN'S CLOTHES!

HEY! NOSTALGIA WEEK WAS LAST MONTH! STILL CHECKING OUT THE *RETRO* FASHIONS?!
NOT EXACTLY! I'M FOLLOWING MRS. DRUTHERS.
DON'T LOOK NOW, BUT YOU'VE GOT SOME CATTY *SNICKERING* OFF THE PORT BOW.
THAT'S THE PROBLEM, WHEN EVERYONE KNOWS YOU. *EVERYONE* KNOWS YOU. I CAN'T GET ANY PRIVACY.

YOU DON'T MEAN **US**, THOUGH, RIGHT? YOU **LOVE** US!

YOU BET! I'M ACTUALLY **RELIEVED** TO SEE YOU.

BETTER BE! AFTER ALL, WHO CAN BETTER MAKE FUN OF THE DERMATOLOGICALLY CORRECT **DEE-DEE**?

AND SAY **HELPFUL** THINGS LIKE, ISN'T THAT YOUR **SUSPECT** WALKING AWAY?

I CROSSED MY FINGERS HOPING MRS. DRUTHER'S WOULDN'T SEE ME.

BUT I GUESS I ***SHOULD*** HAVE BEEN HOPING THE BUS DRIVER ***DID*** SEE ME.

OR AT LEAST THAT DEIRDRE ***DIDN'T***.
ACK

HA-HA-HA!

SHEESH. WHY NOT TAKE A ***PICTURE***, DEIRDRE?

THANKS! I ***WILL***! HA-HA-HA-HA!

CHEER UP, NANCY! MAYBE SANTA CLAUS WILL LET YOU LEAD HIS ***SLEIGH*** NEXT CHRISTMAS!

NICE LINE, DEE-DEE, DID DADDYKINS PAY FOR ***THAT***, TOO?

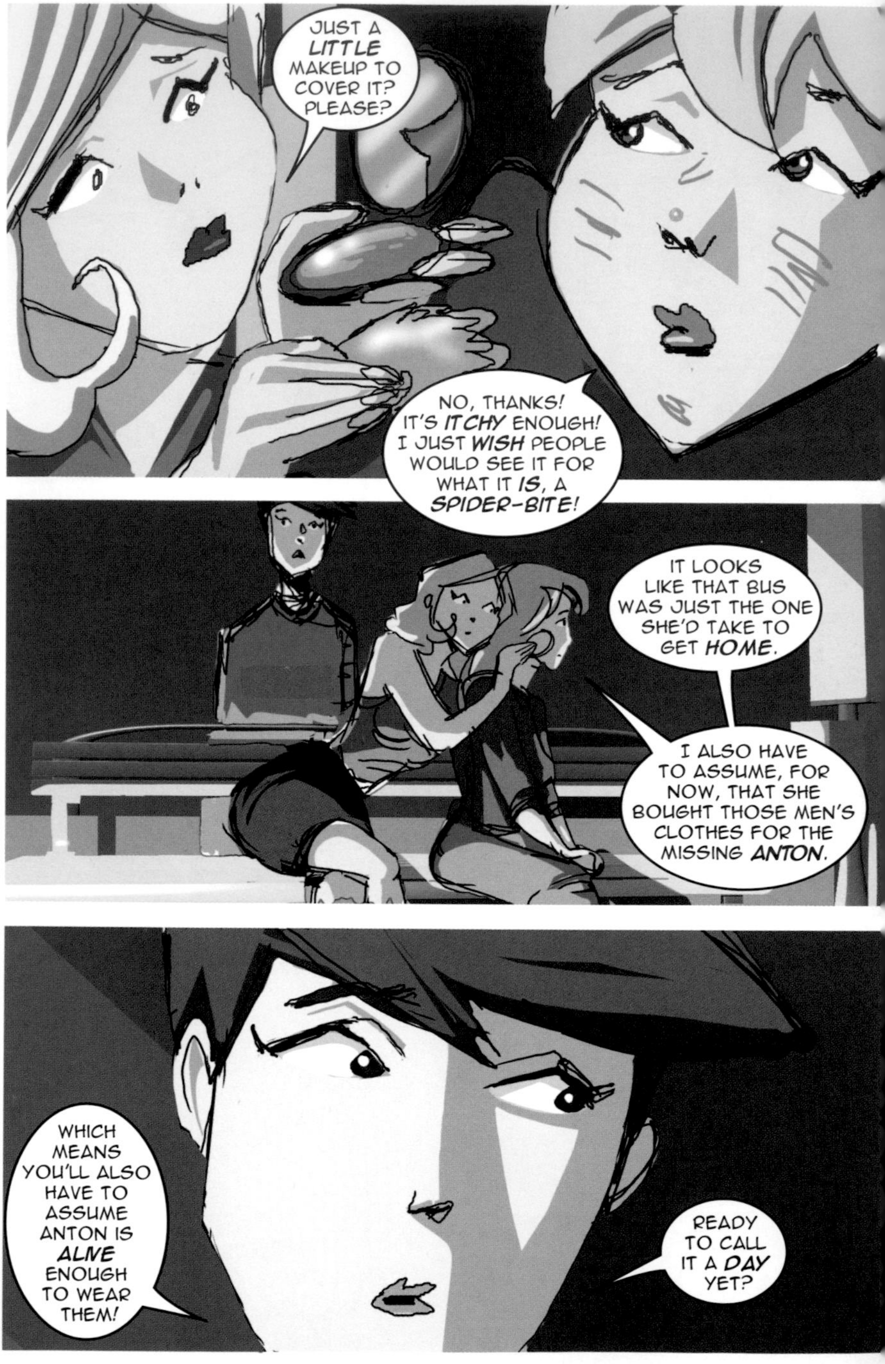

JUST A *LITTLE* MAKEUP TO COVER IT? PLEASE?

NO, THANKS! IT'S *ITCHY* ENOUGH! I JUST *WISH* PEOPLE WOULD SEE IT FOR WHAT IT *IS*, A *SPIDER-BITE*!

IT LOOKS LIKE THAT BUS WAS JUST THE ONE SHE'D TAKE TO GET *HOME*.

I ALSO HAVE TO ASSUME, FOR NOW, THAT SHE BOUGHT THOSE MEN'S CLOTHES FOR THE MISSING *ANTON*.

NOPE!
SHE STILL MIGHT MAKE A STOP SOMEWHERE ALONG THIS ROUTE.

AND I DON'T HAVE TO STOP, SO, I'M BOUND TO CATCH UP IF I FOLLOW THE SAME ROUTE.
COME WITH?
YOU BET!

I DON'T KNOW WHAT I'D DO WITHOUT YOU TWO.
PROBABLY MAKE A RIGHT INSTEAD OF A LEFT UP AHEAD, FOR STARTERS!

TIME PASSED AND WE STILL HADN'T MANAGED TO CATCH UP TO THE BUS.
I WAS STARTING TO THINK IT HAD VANISHED LIKE MR. DRUTHERS!

THERE IT IS!
SCREECH

SOMEONE'S GETTING OFF!
IT'S NOT HER! GEE, I HOPE SHE'S STILL ON THE BUS!

DON'T TELL ME, LET ME GUESS!
YOU STOOD ME UP FOR OUR ROLLER-BLADING DATE BECAUSE YOU THREE ARE ON A CASE, RIGHT?

UM? NO, AND IT'S A SPIDER-BITE.
ACTUALLY I'M FOLLOWING MRS. DRUTHERS, WHO'S IN THAT BUS!
SORRY! GOTTA GO!

I SOMETIMES WONDER IF OTHER GIRL DETECTIVES HAVE PATIENT, UNDERSTANDING BOYFRIENDS.
AS I ZOOMED AWAY WITHOUT EXPLAINING, I HOPED MINE STILL WAS.
GOOD LUCK!
I'D MAKE IT UP TO HIM LATER.

MEANWHILE, NOW THAT I HAD THE BUS, I DIDN'T WANT TO LOSE IT.
OP
WE TAILED IT ALL THE WAY TO SOME OF THE QUIET COUNTRY STREETS THAT SURROUND RIVER HEIGHTS PROPER.

AND I GUESS I GOT A LITTLE TOO ENTHUSIASTIC ABOUT STAYING CLOSE BEHIND!
NANCY, STOP!
SCREECH

CATCH THE BUS IS JUST A FIGURE OF SPEECH!
SORRY.
REMIND ME TO CHECK YOUR BRAKE FLUID, RIGHT AFTER I FIX MY HAIR!

THERE SHE WAS. WE HADN'T LOST HER.

SHE TOOK A NARROW TRAIL THROUGH SOME PRETTY THICK WOODS.
WHICH MEANT WE HAD TO FOLLOW ON FOOT.

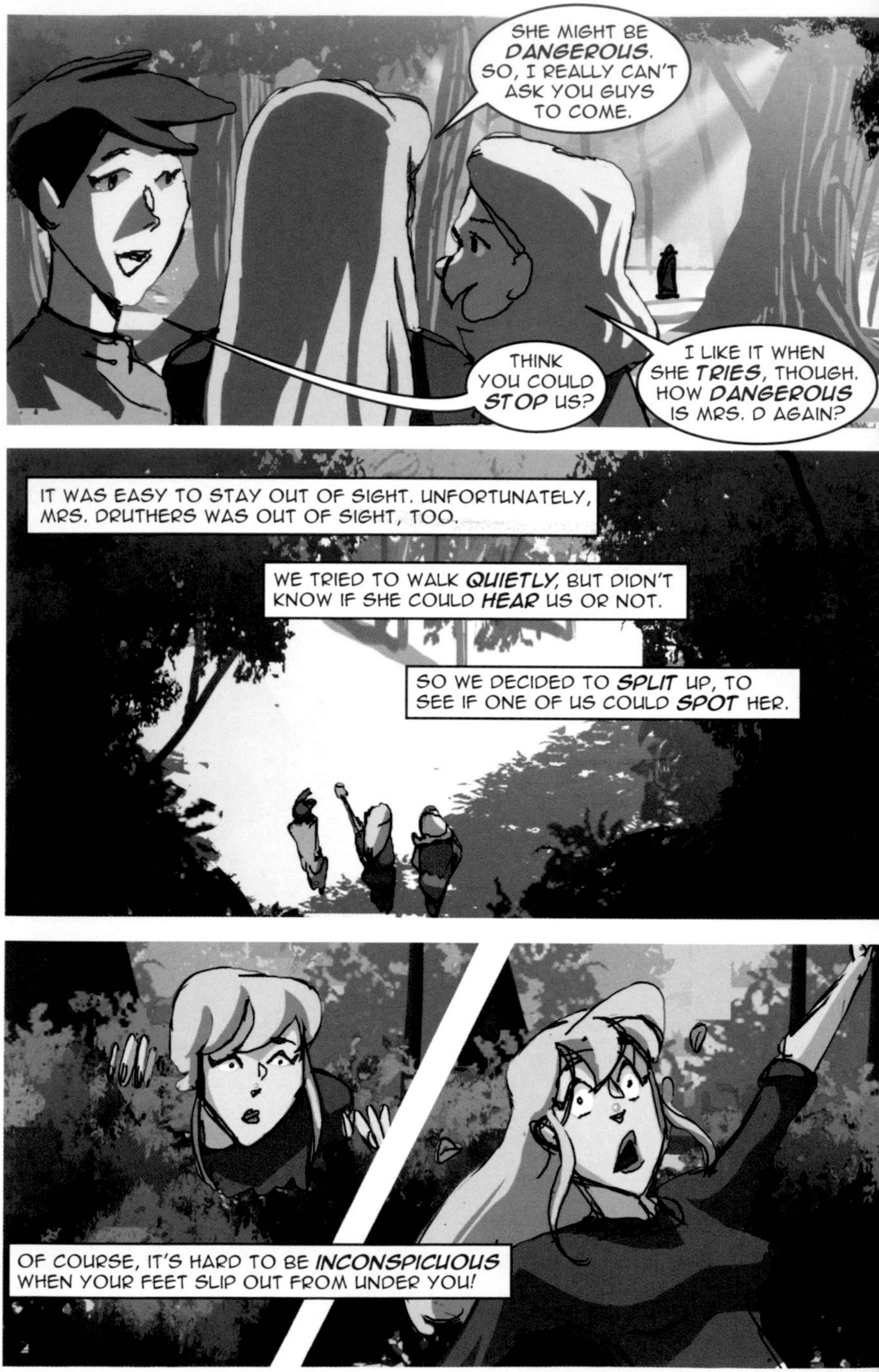

SHE MIGHT BE *DANGEROUS*. SO, I REALLY CAN'T ASK YOU GUYS TO COME.

THINK YOU COULD *STOP* US?

I LIKE IT WHEN SHE *TRIES*, THOUGH. HOW *DANGEROUS* IS MRS. D AGAIN?

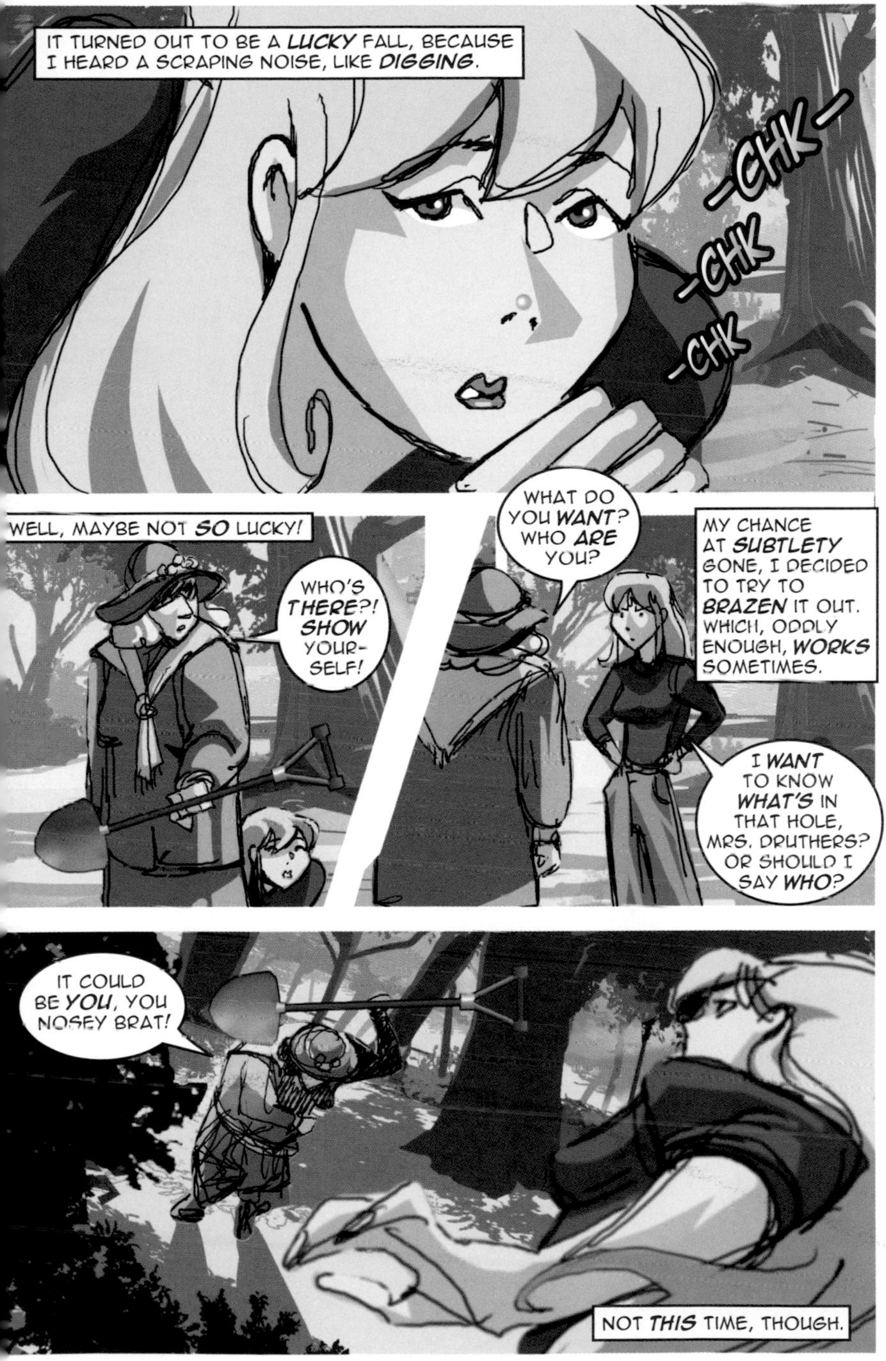

IT TURNED OUT TO BE A ***LUCKY*** FALL, BECAUSE I HEARD A SCRAPING NOISE, LIKE ***DIGGING***.

-CHK-

-CHK

-CHK

WELL, MAYBE NOT ***SO*** LUCKY!

WHO'S ***THERE***?! ***SHOW*** YOURSELF!

WHAT DO YOU ***WANT***? WHO ***ARE*** YOU?

MY CHANCE AT ***SUBTLETY*** GONE, I DECIDED TO TRY TO ***BRAZEN*** IT OUT. WHICH, ODDLY ENOUGH, ***WORKS*** SOMETIMES.

I ***WANT*** TO KNOW ***WHAT'S*** IN THAT HOLE, MRS. DRUTHERS? OR SHOULD I SAY ***WHO***?

HEY, WATCH WHERE YOU POINT THAT THING! IT MIGHT BE LOADED!
WHAT DO YOU WANT WITH ME?! CAN'T A WOMAN DIG A HOLE WITHOUT BEING ACCOSTED ANYMORE?
WE JUST WANT TO KNOW WHAT HAPPENED TO YOUR HUSBAND, MRS. DRUTHERS. MAYBE WE SHOULD FINISH THAT DIGGING YOU STARTED.
LET'S CALL THE POLICE FIRST, NANCY. LET THEM DO THE DIGGING.
GOOD IDEA, BESS-- OOOMF!
NO!

MAN, SHE'S STRONG FOR AN OLD WOMAN!
CAN WE PLEASE LET THE COPS CATCH HER?
HEY, GUYS! LOOK!

THESE ALL BELONG TO ANTON DRUTHERS! THE SAFETY DEPOSIT BOX MUST HAVE HAD THE KEY FOR THIS. BUT WHY BURY HIS PERSONAL EFFECTS?
MAYBE 'CAUSE SHE KILLED HIM AND DIDN'T WANT THE MEMORY OF HIM AROUND THE HOUSE, BUT THEY WERE TOO PRECIOUS TO JUST THROW OUT?!

MAYBE, BUT IT'S STRANGE SHE'D SAVE HIS PASSPORT AND AN OLD HAT AND NOT HIS WEDDING RING OR WALLET!
I'M CALLING CHIEF McGINNIS TO MEET US AT HER HOUSE WITH A WARRANT. MY GUESS IS SHE'S RUSHING HOME TO HIDE EVIDENCE.

UH, BATTERIES ARE DEAD IN BOTH MINE AND YOUR SPARE CELL, GEORGE!
GOOD THING YOU HAVE MORE THAN ONE FRIEND!

I WASN'T SURE WHAT TO EXPECT AT THE DRUTHERS, SO WE WERE GLAD TO SEE CHIEF McGINNIS HAD GOTTEN THERE AHEAD OF US.
ONE THING I DID NOT EXPECT WAS...

...MR. DRUTHERS!
END CHAPTER TWO

CHAPTER THREE: THE HEIR TRANSPARENT
NANCY DREW, WOULD YOU CARE TO EXPLAIN WHY I CHASED DOWN A JUDGE FOR A SEARCH WARRANT WHEN YOUR SUPPOSED MURDER VICTIM IS STILL ALIVE?
I'M TOLD THERE COMES A MOMENT IN EVERY DETECTIVE'S CAREER WHEN IT TURNS OUT THEIR STRONGEST HUNCHES JUST TURN OUT TO BE WRONG.
AND THEN THE ONLY THING YOU CAN DO IS SAY...
UM.... OOPS?

BUT, HONESTLY, I STILL COULDN'T BELIEVE IT!
OOPS? YOU HOODLUMS TERRORIZED MY WIFE TODAY! IF IT'S ANY OF YOUR BUSINESS AT ALL, I'VE BEEN OUT OF THE COUNTRY HELPING A SICK BROTHER!
BUT YOU'RE BACK NOW, AND YOU'RE ALL RIGHT?
I HAD TO COME BACK TO CLAIM MY INHERITANCE. AND IF CHIEF McGINNIS HADN'T VOUCHED FOR YOU, I'D BE PRESSING HARASSMENT CHARGES RIGHT NOW!
SATISFIED, NANCY? DOES MR. DRUTHERS SEEM NOT DEAD ENOUGH TO YOU?

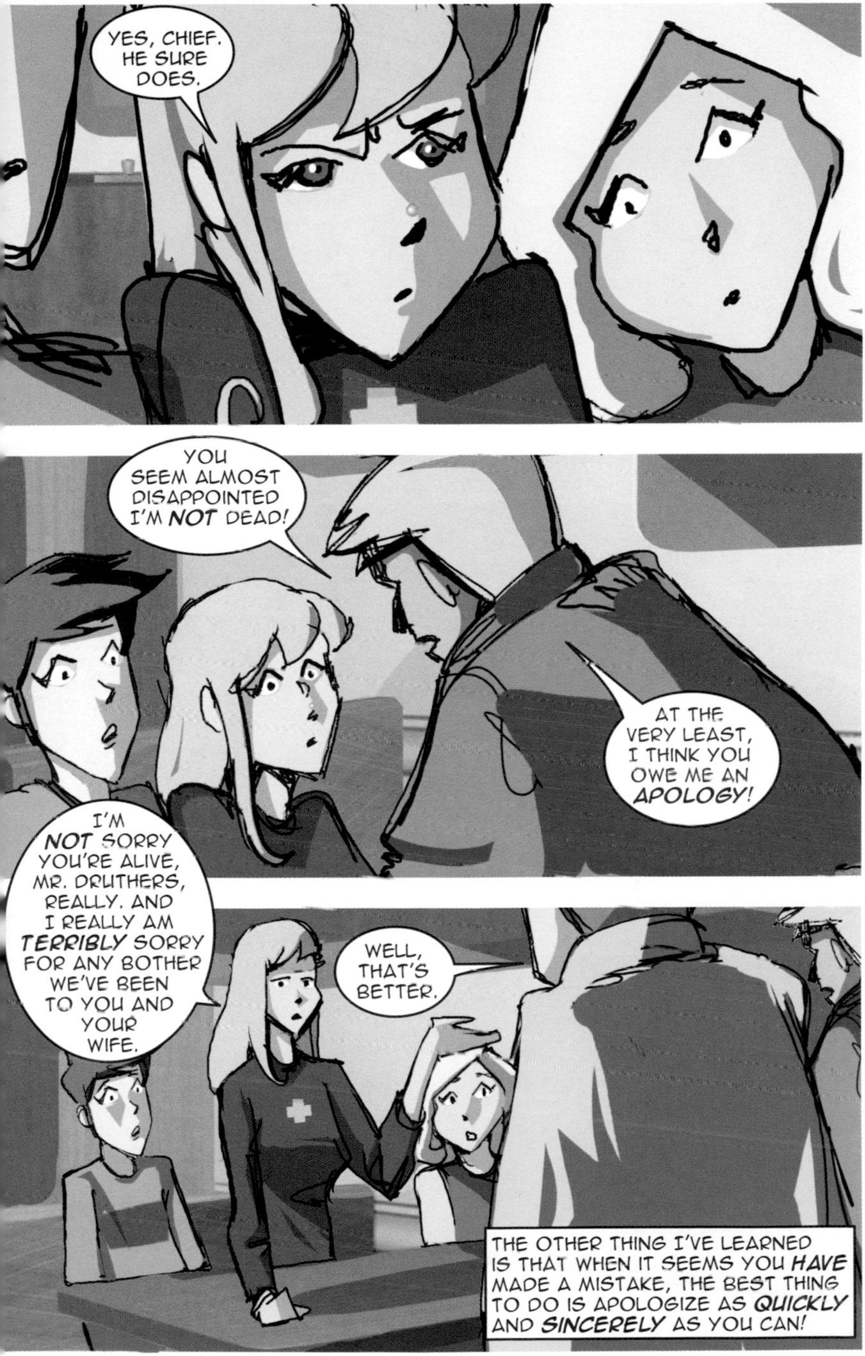

YOU SEEM ALMOST DISAPPOINTED I'M ***NOT*** DEAD!

AT THE VERY LEAST, I THINK YOU OWE ME AN ***APOLOGY***!

I'M ***NOT*** SORRY YOU'RE ALIVE, MR. DRUTHERS, REALLY. AND I REALLY AM ***TERRIBLY*** SORRY FOR ANY BOTHER WE'VE BEEN TO YOU AND YOUR WIFE.

WELL, THAT'S BETTER.

THE OTHER THING I'VE LEARNED IS THAT WHEN IT SEEMS YOU ***HAVE*** MADE A MISTAKE, THE BEST THING TO DO IS APOLOGIZE AS ***QUICKLY*** AND ***SINCERELY*** AS YOU CAN!

WOW, I CAN'T BELIEVE IT! THE FAMOUS NANCY INTUITION HAS COME UP *EMPTY*! THAT'S A FIRST!
GUESS YOU'VE GIVEN UP ON THIS CASE NOW, HUH?

HAVEN'T YOU?

WELL... NOPE!
SEE, APOLOGIZE *QUICKLY*, AND YOU CAN GET BACK ON THE CASE EVEN *FASTER*!

IN THIS CASE, THAT MEANT HEADING TO THE RIVER HEIGHTS CITY HALL TO CHECK ON THE PUBLIC BIRTH RECORDS.
UNFORTUNATELY, SOME OF THE OLDER RECORDS WEREN'T EVEN ON *COMPUTER*!
BUT WITH BESS AND GEORGE HELPING, I MANAGED TO COVER THE FILES IN ONE THIRD THE TIME!
THAT *PROVES* IT!
UNLESS HE'S OVER A HUNDRED AND TWENTY OR LESS THAN TWO DAYS OLD...
...MR. DRUTHERS DOESN'T *HAVE* A BROTHER! SO HE *COULDN'T* HAVE BEEN AWAY VISITING HIM!
SOMETHING CROOKED'S GOING ON BACK AT THAT TRAILER, AND *I'M* GOING TO FIND OUT WHAT IT IS!

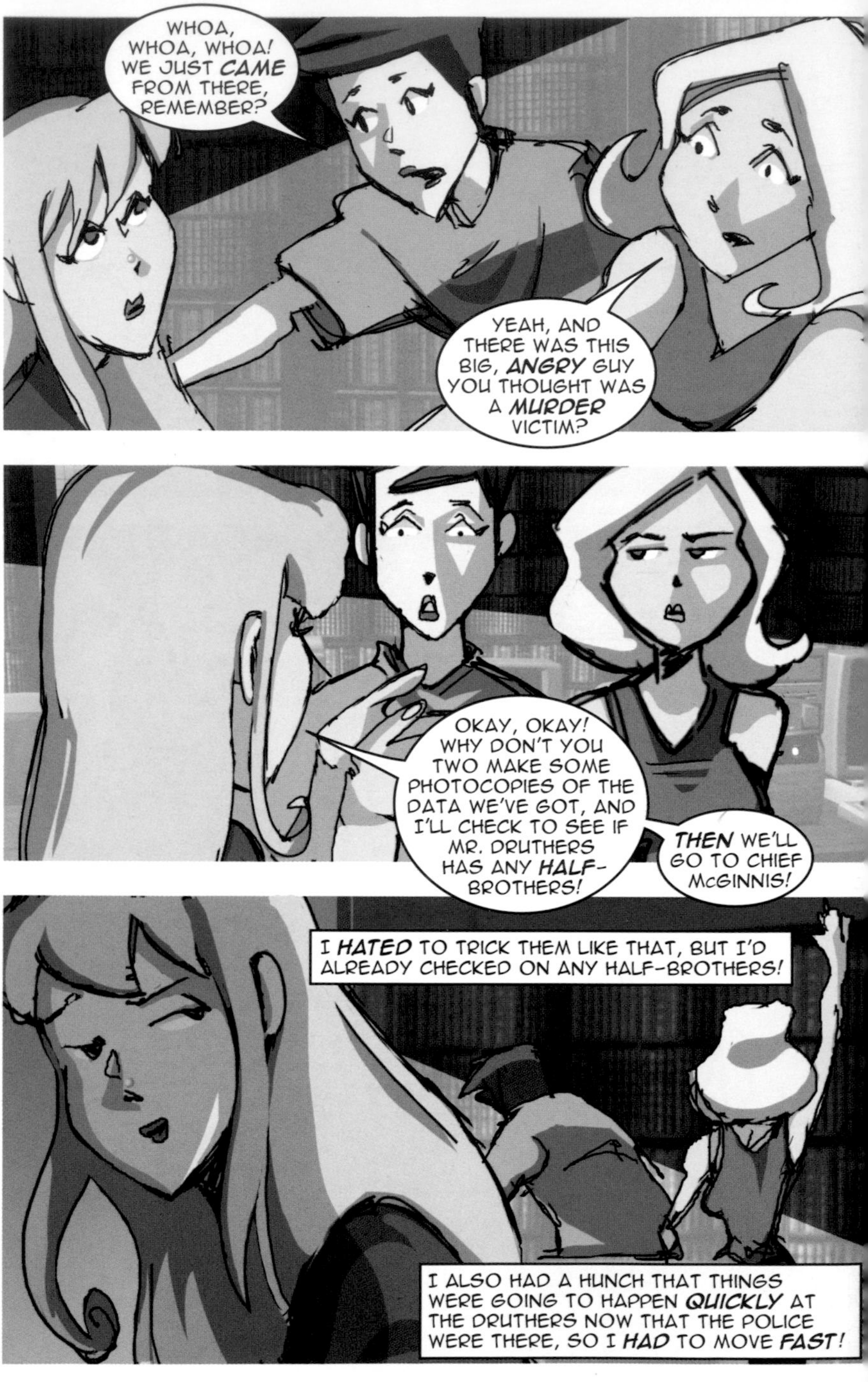

WHOA, WHOA, WHOA! WE JUST CAME FROM THERE, REMEMBER?

YEAH, AND THERE WAS THIS BIG, ANGRY GUY YOU THOUGHT WAS A MURDER VICTIM?

I PARKED MY CAR A HALF MILE AWAY, AND *HID* IT UNDER SOME BRUSH.
THE PLACE SEEMED EMPTY WHEN I ARRIVED, SO IT WAS A *PERFECT* CHANCE TO SEARCH FOR CLUES.

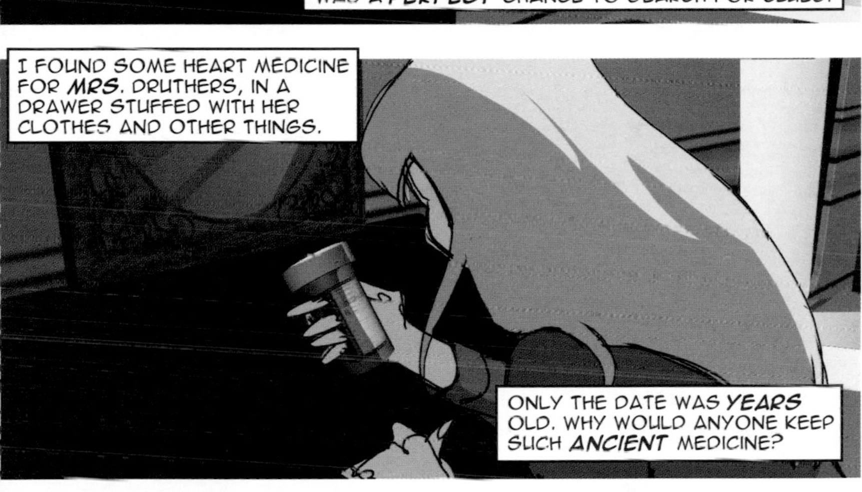
I FOUND SOME HEART MEDICINE FOR *MRS*. DRUTHERS, IN A DRAWER STUFFED WITH HER CLOTHES AND OTHER THINGS.
ONLY THE DATE WAS *YEARS* OLD. WHY WOULD ANYONE KEEP SUCH *ANCIENT* MEDICINE?

THEN, WHEN I SAW MY SPIDER-BITTEN NOSE IN A MIRROR, THE ONE THAT LOOKED JUST LIKE A *PIMPLE*, I REALIZED *EXACTLY* WHAT HAD BEEN GOING ON.

MY HAPPY FEELING AT SOLVING THE CASE WAS SHORT-LIVED.
BECAUSE I HEARD SOMEONE MUMBLING OUTSIDE.
I WASN'T ALONE.

AS I GOT CLOSER, I REALIZED IT WASN'T MUMBLING AT ALL. IT HAD MORE A PLEADING, SING-SONG QUALITY...

... LIKE PRAYING.

THERE WAS MR. DRUTHERS, LOOKING VERY SOLEMN, SITTING ON A SMALL SPOT OF LAND IN THE WOODS RIGHT BEHIND HIS TRAILER.

I WONDERED WHY I HADN'T ***NOTICED*** IT BEFORE, THEN REALIZED MAYBE HE KEPT IT COVERED OVER WITH BRUSH.

IT LOOKED VERY NEAT AND CLEAN NOW.

LIKE A ***GRAVESITE.***

I ALSO HAD A FEELING THAT THE LITTLE PLOT OF LAND HAD ALL THE *PROOF* I NEEDED TO CLOSE THIS CASE.

SO I SLIPPED OUT FOR A CLOSER LOOK.

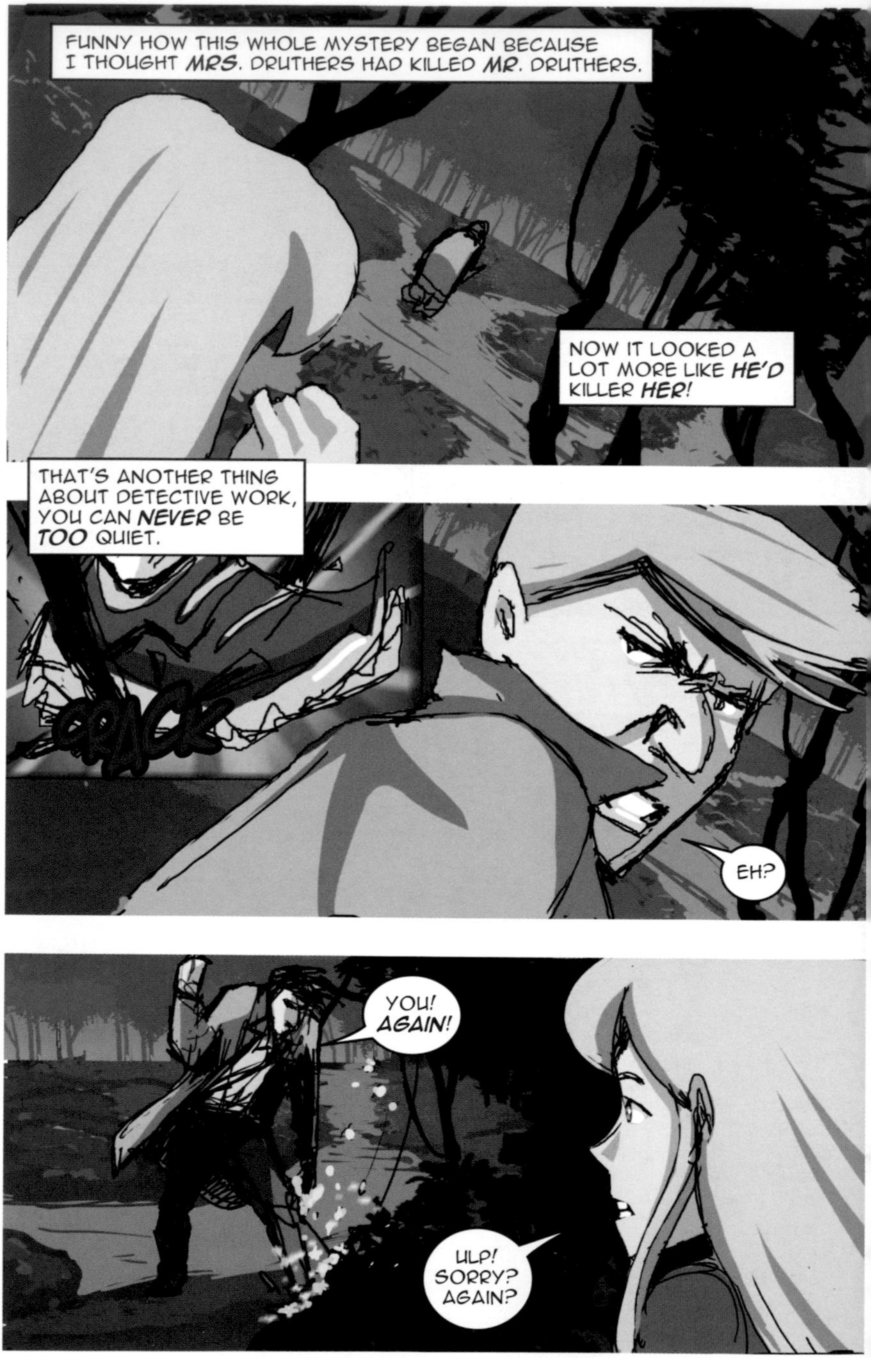

FUNNY HOW THIS WHOLE MYSTERY BEGAN BECAUSE I THOUGHT ***MRS***. DRUTHERS HAD KILLED ***MR***. DRUTHERS.

NOW IT LOOKED A LOT MORE LIKE ***HE'D*** KILLER ***HER!***

THAT'S ANOTHER THING ABOUT DETECTIVE WORK, YOU CAN ***NEVER*** BE ***TOO*** QUIET.

CRACK

EH?

Y'KNOW, YOU THINK I'D BE USED TO THIS SORT OF THING BY NOW.
I MEAN, I HIDE A LOT DURING MY CASES. USUALLY, I DON'T GET CAUGHT, BUT HEY, SOMETIMES I DO.
SO, YOU'D THINK I'D BE PREPARED, THAT AT LEAST MY HEART WOULDN'T LEAP INTO MY THROAT WITH FEAR, OR MY KNEES WOULDN'T SHAKE SO MUCH.
BUT, I GUESS SOME THINGS, NO MATTER HOW OFTEN THEY HAPPEN, STILL FEEL LIKE THE FIRST TIME!

WHY WON'T YOU JUST LEAVE US ALONE?
HE HAD A POINT, SORT OF. I DON'T LIKE BOTHERING ANYONE. BUT I HAD REASON TO BELIEVE A CRIME HAD BEEN COMMITTED.

AND NOW, I WAS SURE OF IT!
OKAY, SO MAYBE IT WASN'T THE CRIME I ORIGINALLY THOUGHT IT WAS, BUT IT WAS STILL A CRIME!

GASP

I'D HAD SO MUCH TROUBLE WITH THE ONE SPIDER BITE, I STARTED RUNNING AND SWATTING AT THE SAME TIME.

OF COURSE, WHEN YOU DO TWO THINGS AT ONCE, YOU CAN NEVER GIVE EITHER YOUR FULL ATTENTION...
I GUESS I WAS PAYING MORE ATTENTION TO THE SWATTING!

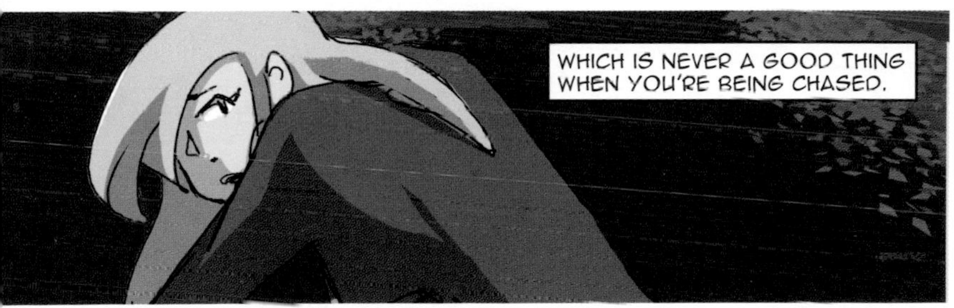
WHICH IS NEVER A GOOD THING WHEN YOU'RE BEING CHASED.

UM... WOULD IT HELP IF I SAID I WAS REALLY, REALLY SORRY?

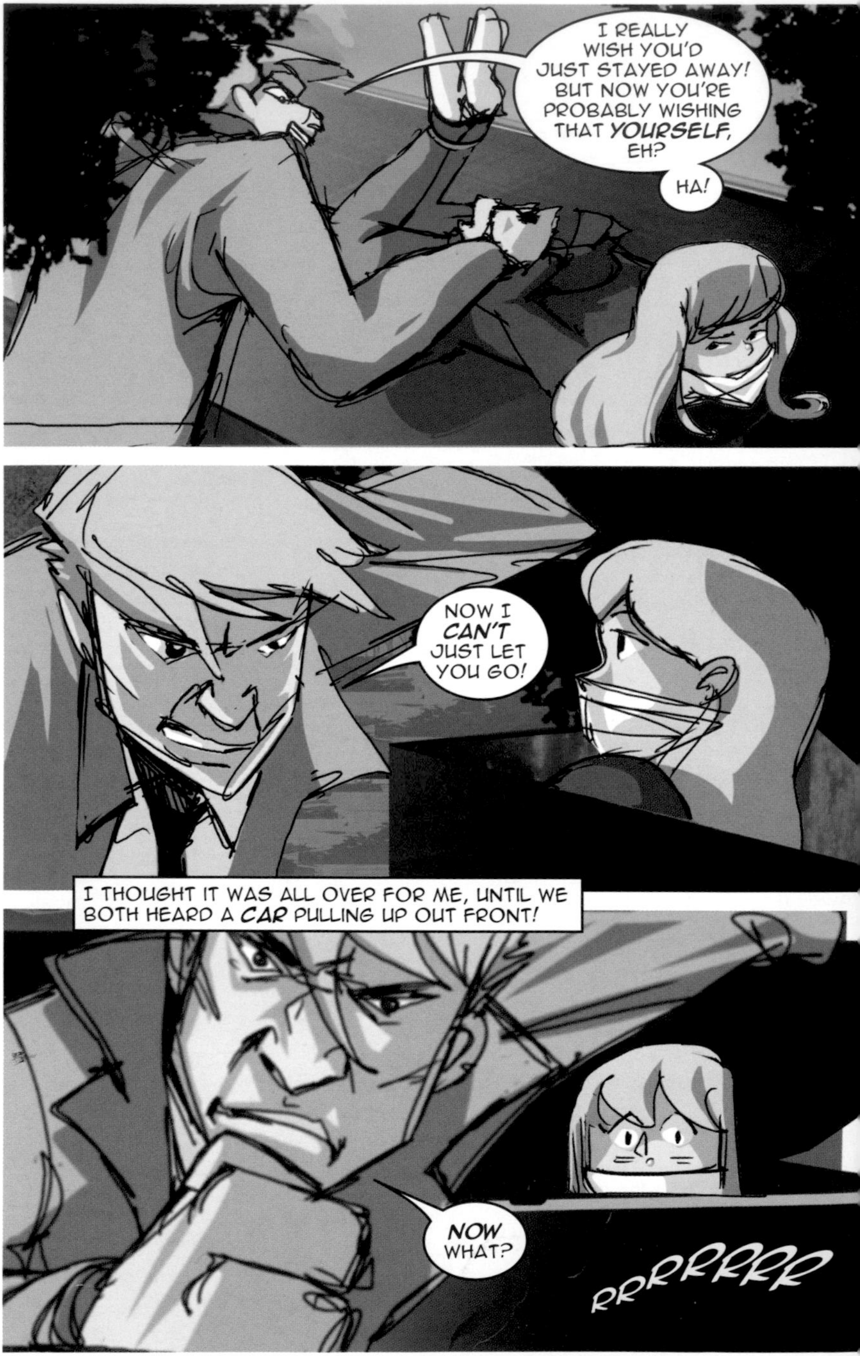

NOW I *CAN'T* JUST LET YOU GO!

I THOUGHT IT WAS ALL OVER FOR ME, UNTIL WE BOTH HEARD A *CAR* PULLING UP OUT FRONT!

NOW WHAT?

RRRRRRRR

IT WAS MY DAD. I KNOW A LOT OF GIRLS GET UPSET WHEN THEIR PARENTS INTERFERE IN THEIR LIVES, BUT, BOY, I WAS THRILLED TO SEE HIM.
HIS TIMING COULDN'T HAVE BEEN BETTER!
NOW IF ONLY HE KNEW WHERE I WAS!
YOU KEEP QUIET IF YOU KNOW WHAT'S GOOD FOR YOU!
YEAH, WELL, I DID KNOW WHAT WAS GOOD FOR ME, AND IT DIDN'T INCLUDE BEING TIED UP IN A STORAGE COMPARTMENT!
ESPECIALLY WITH SPIDERS.

MR. DRUTHERS? I'M CARSON DREW.
THE ATTORNEY HANDLING JAKE AND AMELIA'S WILL. YES, MY WIFE TOLD ME. SHE'S... NOT HERE AT THE MOMENT.

WELL, THE FORMS ALL CHECKED OUT, SO I'M JUST HERE TO DELIVER YOUR INHERITANCE.
THEY'RE... LOVELY. MY COUSINS ALWAYS HAD GREAT TASTE.

I JUST NEED YOU TO SIGN THIS RECEIPT, AND I'LL BE ON MY WAY!
CERTAINLY.

FUNNY ABOUT THAT LAKE JUST *VANISHING*, EH?
BY LEANING AGAINST THE TRAILER, I COULD HEAR EVERY WORD. JUDGING FROM THE **PLEASANT** CONVERSATION, MY DAD HAD NO **CLUE** WHERE I WAS.

SERVES ME ***RIGHT*** FOR HIDING MY CAR IN THE BRUSH AND ***WALKING***! SOMETIMES, I OUTSMART MYSELF!
THE PROBLEM NOW WAS, HOW TO GET HIM A ***MESSAGE***?

WHEN I WAS JUST A LITTLE GIRL, MY FATHER TAUGHT ME ***MORSE CODE***.
THE SIMPLEST MESSAGE YOU CAN SEND IS A CALL FOR HELP, SOS, WHICH IS THREE SHORT TAPS, THREE LONG TAPS, THEN THREE SHORT ONES AGAIN.

WHAT'S THAT CLICKING NOISE?
TAP-TAP-TAP TAP. TAP. TAP. TAP-TAP-TAP

OH, IT'S UH... THOSE LOUSY PIPES. BAD HEATING, YOU KNOW.
WELL, THE RECEIPT'S SIGNED. THANKS SO MUCH FOR COMING BY!

YOU CAN PROBABLY AFFORD MUCH BETTER PLUMBING NOW!
BEST OF LUCK TO YOU AND YOUR WIFE!

I KNEW MY DAD HAD HEARD ME. HE HAD TO.
HE WAS JUST WAITING FOR THE RIGHT MOMENT TO COME AND FREE ME!

AND... AND... HE WAS JUST SHAKING HANDS WITH MR. DRUTHERS TO LULL HIM INTO A FALSE SENSE OF SECURITY.
YEAH, THAT WAS IT.

ONLY THEN, HE DROVE AWAY!
WHICH MEANT ~ULP~ MAYBE HE DIDN'T GET THE MESSAGE!

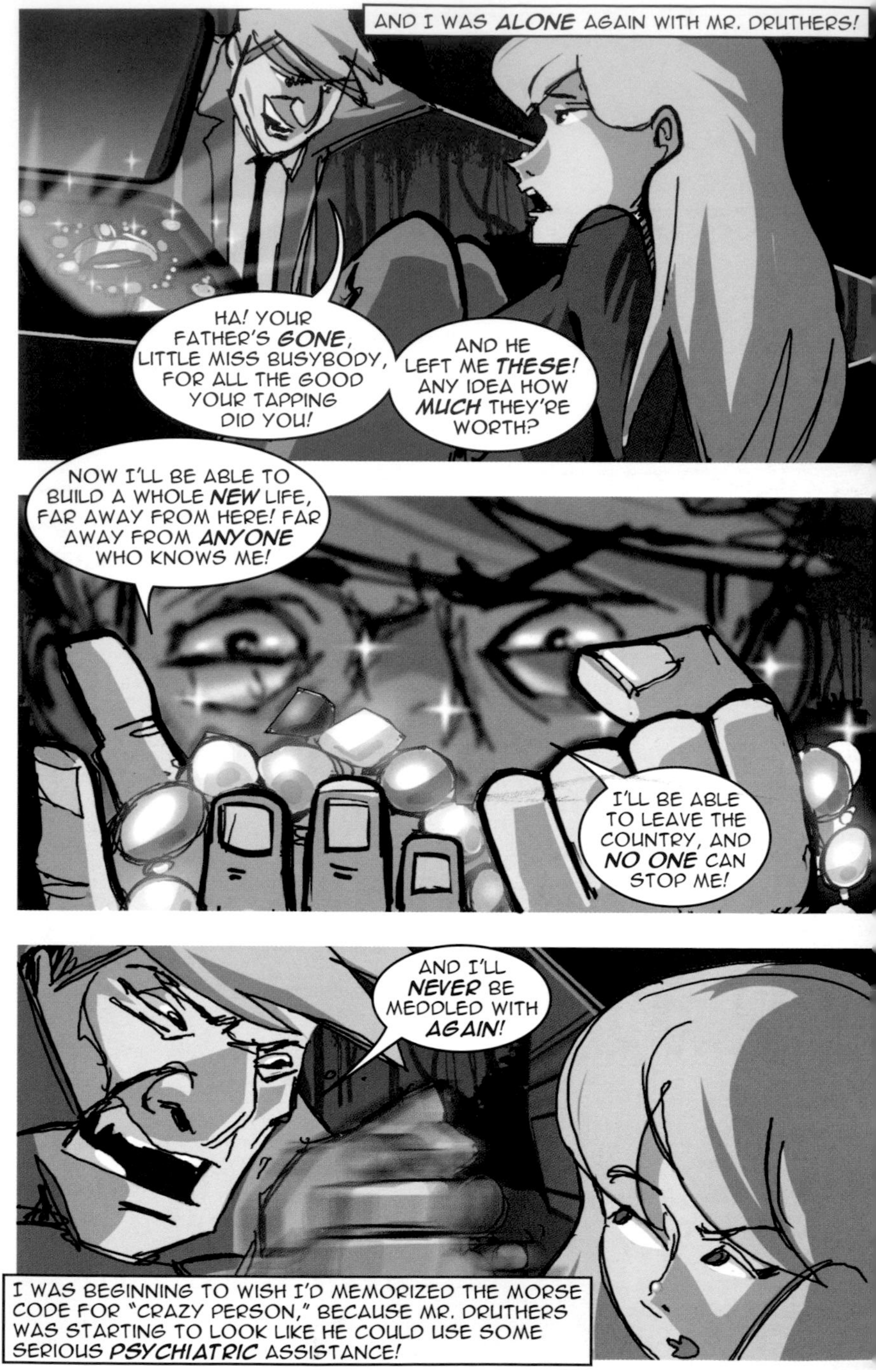

AND I WAS *ALONE* AGAIN WITH MR. DRUTHERS!

HA! YOUR FATHER'S *GONE*, LITTLE MISS BUSYBODY, FOR ALL THE GOOD YOUR TAPPING DID YOU!

AND HE LEFT ME *THESE*! ANY IDEA HOW *MUCH* THEY'RE WORTH?

NOW I'LL BE ABLE TO BUILD A WHOLE *NEW* LIFE, FAR AWAY FROM HERE! FAR AWAY FROM *ANYONE* WHO KNOWS ME!

I'LL BE ABLE TO LEAVE THE COUNTRY, AND *NO ONE* CAN STOP ME!

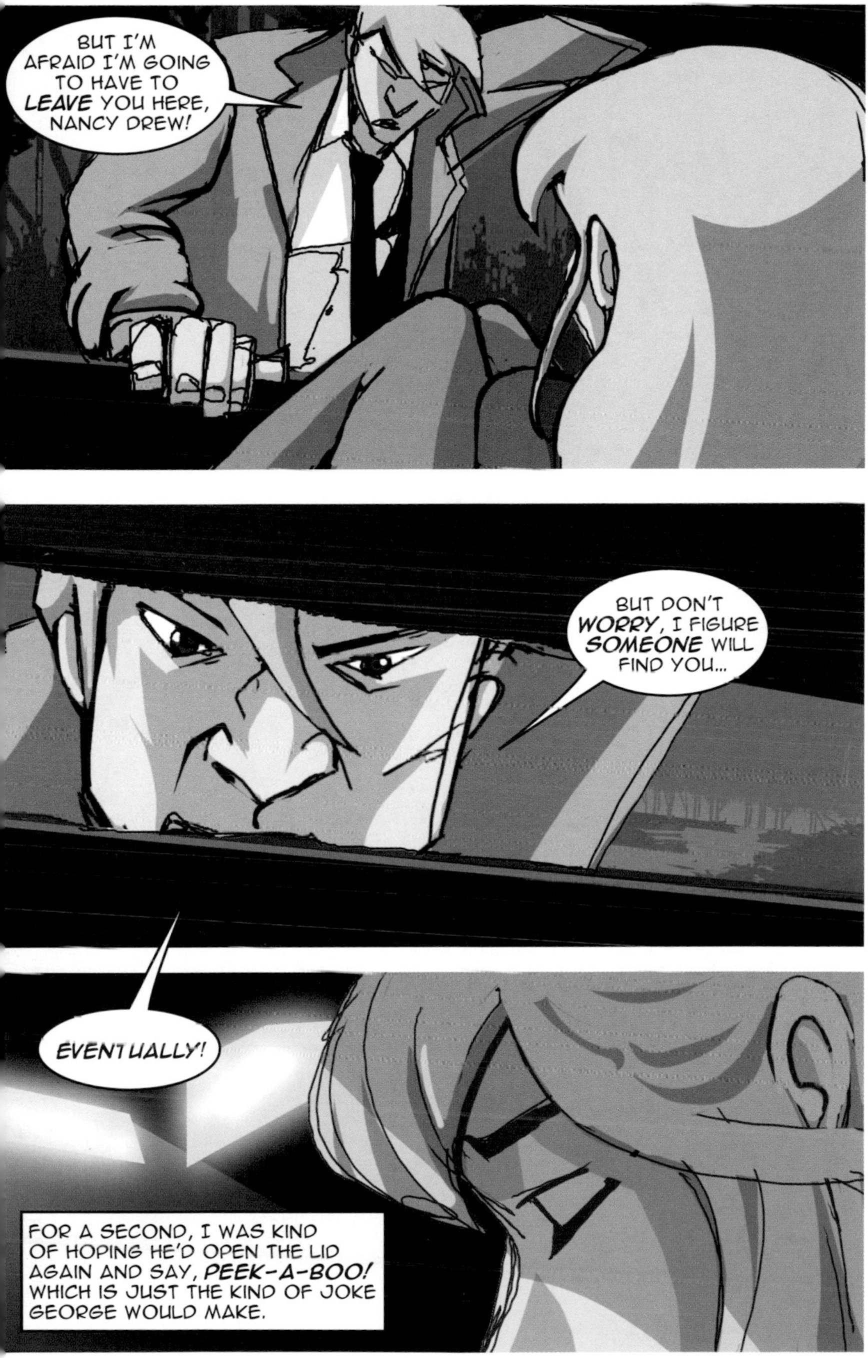

BUT DON'T WORRY, I FIGURE SOMEONE WILL FIND YOU...

EVENTUALLY!

FOR A SECOND, I WAS KIND OF HOPING HE'D OPEN THE LID AGAIN AND SAY, PEEK-A-BOO! WHICH IS JUST THE KIND OF JOKE GEORGE WOULD MAKE.

BUT HE DIDN'T. HE JUST WENT INSIDE, TO *PACK* I FIGURED.
I WONDERED IF TELLING HIM I *KNEW* HIS *SECRET* WOULD HAVE MADE ANY DIFFERENCE

IT PROBABLY WOULD HAVE JUST MADE HIM MORE *ANGRY*.
WOULD THIS REALLY BE *IT* FOR ME? LEFT ALL ALONE TIED UP IN THE *DARK*?

I WANTED TO BELIEVE SOMEONE WOULD FIND ME, BUT THE *LONGER* I WAITED, THE *HARDER* IT WAS TO BELIEVE.
AFTER A *WHILE*, I WAS STARTING TO FEEL LIKE MAYBE I WOULD JUST VANISH FOREVER, LIKE THE *LAKE*!

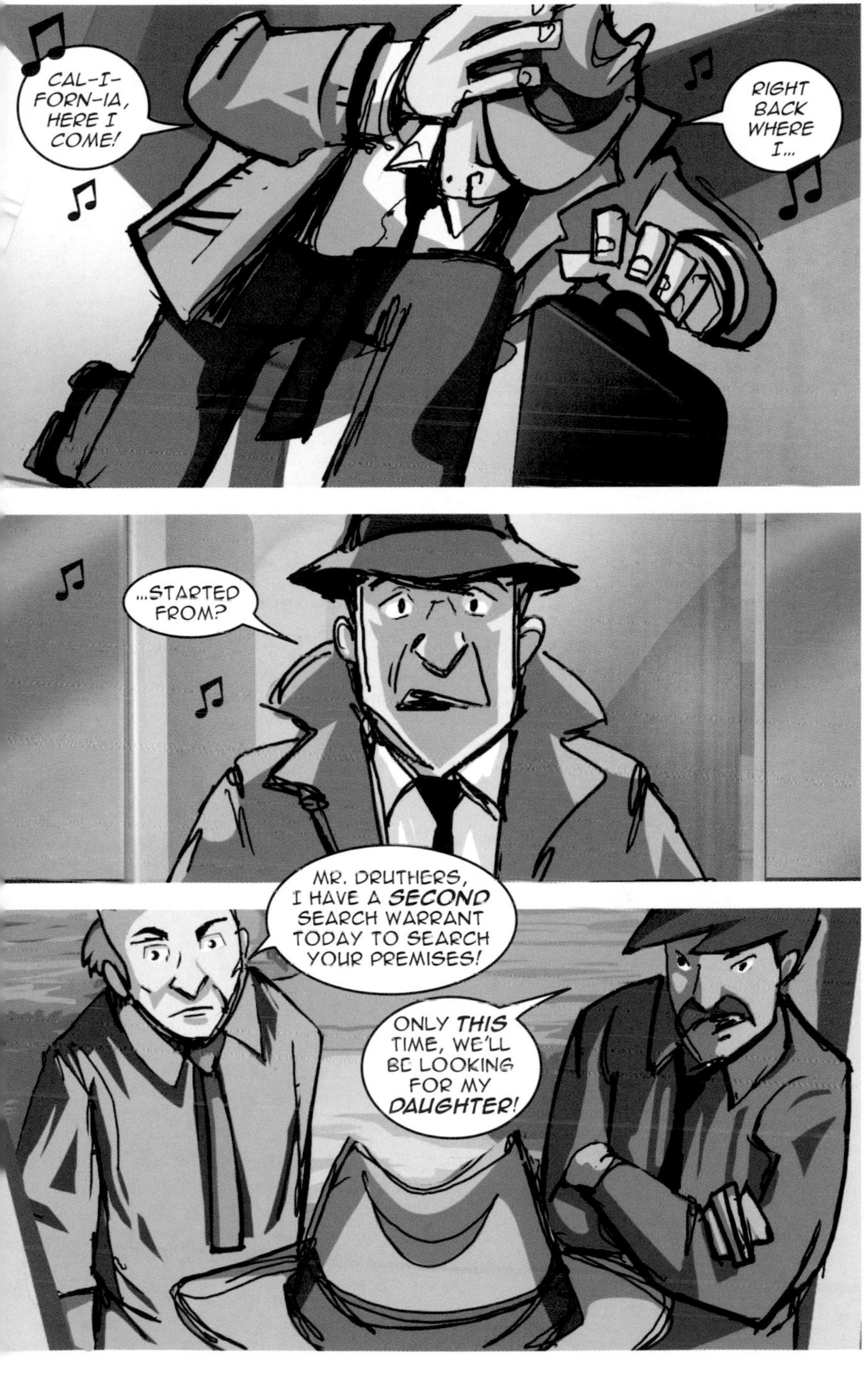

CAL-I-FORN-IA, HERE I COME!
RIGHT BACK WHERE I...

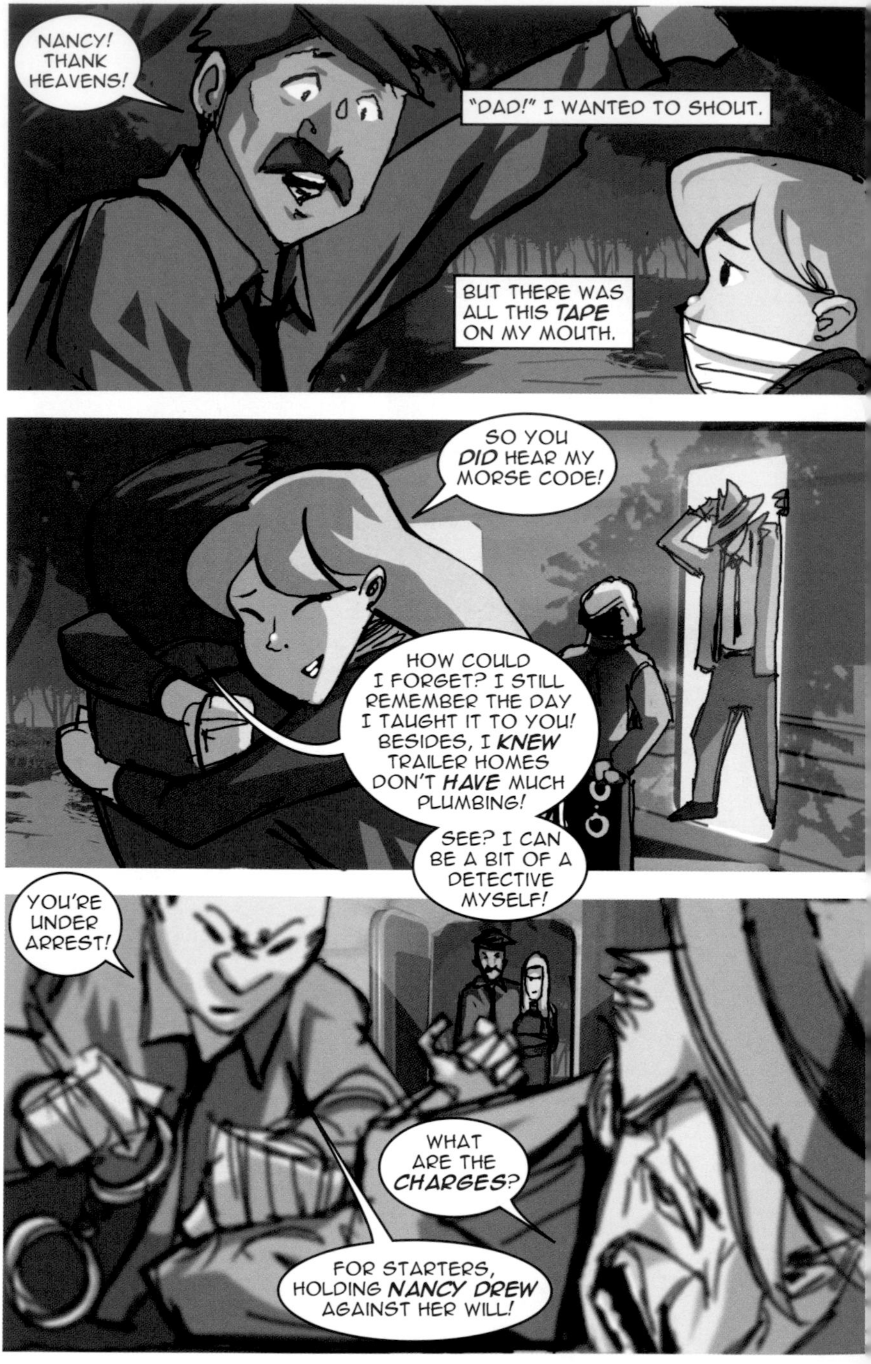

SO YOU *DID* HEAR MY MORSE CODE!

HOW COULD I FORGET? I STILL REMEMBER THE DAY I TAUGHT IT TO YOU! BESIDES, I *KNEW* TRAILER HOMES DON'T *HAVE* MUCH PLUMBING!

SEE? I CAN BE A BIT OF A DETECTIVE MYSELF!

YOU'RE UNDER ARREST!

WHAT ARE THE *CHARGES*?

FOR STARTERS, HOLDING *NANCY DREW* AGAINST HER WILL!

AND POSSIBLY FOR KILLING MRS. DRUTHERS! WHERE IS SHE?

NO, DAD. HE DIDN'T KILL HER, AND SHE DIDN'T KILL HIM! I WAS WRONG ABOUT THAT PART, ANYWAY!
WHAT? THEN WHERE IS SHE?

WELL, IF YOU EAN THE WOMAN HO CAME TO OUR HOUSE...
HE IS MRS. DRUTHERS!

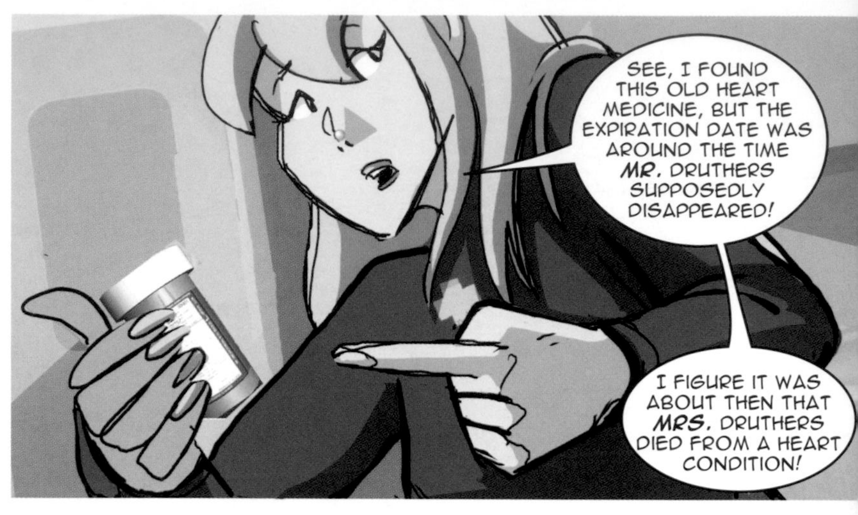
SEE, I FOUND THIS OLD HEART MEDICINE, BUT THE EXPIRATION DATE WAS AROUND THE TIME MR. DRUTHERS SUPPOSEDLY DISAPPEARED!
I FIGURE IT WAS ABOUT THEN THAT MRS. DRUTHERS DIED FROM A HEART CONDITION!

MR. DRUTHERS WAS VERY POOR, YOU MIGHT EVEN SAY DESPERATE.
SO, TO CONTINUE RECEIVING HER DISABILITY PAYMENTS, HE BEGAN MASQUER-ADING AS HER.

LOOK FAMILIAR?

THAT'S AMAZ-ING!
SINCE HE COULDN'T BE BOTH OF THEM AT ONCE, HE LET PEOPLE THINK HE'D VANISHED.
THE INHERITANCE PRESENTED HIM WITH A QUANDARY THAT WOUND UP UNRAVELING HIS DISGUISE.
A QUANDARY? HA! THE ONLY THING THAT UNRAVELED MY DISGUISE WAS NANCY DREW!
JUST KEEP WALKING, MR. DRUTHERS. OR SHOULD I SAY, MR. AND MRS. DRUTHERS?

A FEW DAYS LATER, THE CITY ANNOUNCED A PLAN TO RESTORE THE LAKE BY UNEARTHING UNDERGROUND STREAMS. WE DECIDED TO GO AND WATCH.
WHO'D'VE THOUGHT STARING AT A MUDDY LAKE BOTTOM COULD BE SO INTERESTING.
WELL, IT'S NOT SOMETHING YOU SEE EVERY DAY
SPEAKING OF WHICH, HOW DID YOU FIGURE OUT MR. DRUTHER'S DISGUISE?
HONESTLY? IT WAS MY SPIDER-BITE!
EVERYONE THOUGHT IT WAS A PIMPLE WHEN IT WASN'T. JUST LIKE EVERY-ONE THOUGHT IT WAS MRS. DRUTHERS, WHEN IT WASN'T.
DAD WAS RIGHT!
IT WAS UNDER MY NOSE THE WHOLE TIME!
THE END

Special Advance Preview of NANCY DREW Graphic Novel #6 – "Mr. Cheeters Is Missing"

... A REALLY LOUD, MESSY SNEEZE FROM ONE OF YOUR BEST FRIENDS.
AH-CHOO!
IN THIS CASE, BESS, OF THE COUSINS, BESS AND GEORGE.
CHAPTER ONE: GOING APE

BLESS YOU!
GEE, BESS, COVER YOUR **NOSE**, WILL YOU? YOU'VE BEEN BLASTING THEM OUT LIKE A **STEAM BOAT** WHISTLE!
THE ONE NEXT TO ME BEING **GEORGE**.

SORRY, GUYS! THEY KIND OF **SNEAK** UP ON ME! MY **ALLERGIES** ARE JUST GETTING WORSE AND **WORSE**.
MY TESTS ARE DUE BACK FROM THE LAB SOON, BUT MY **DOCTOR** ALREADY THINKS I HAVE TO GET **RID** OF...
...**RID** OF...

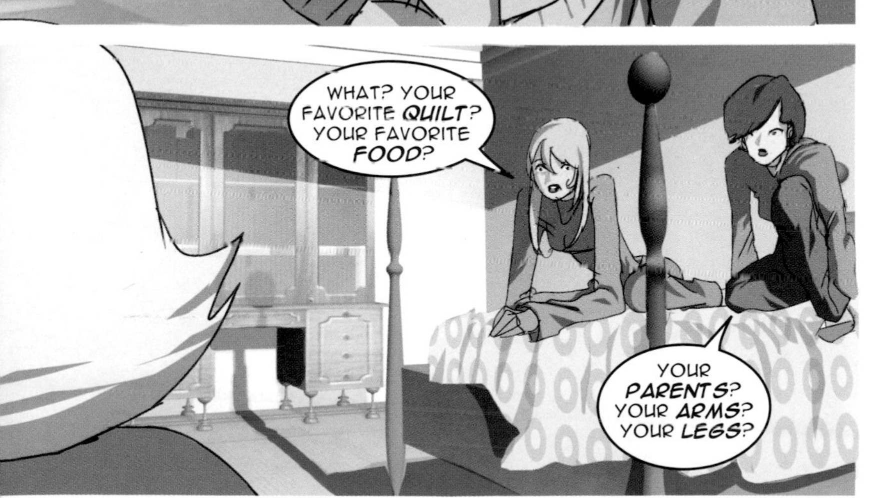

NO, MY STUFFED TOYS! I COLLECT THEM, AND THEY COLLECT DUST!
I KNOW YOU'LL THINK IT'S SILLY, BUT I'VE HAD SOME OF THEM SINCE I WAS LITTLE! THEY'RE LIKE FAMILY, PRACTICALLY!
ACTUALLY, IT'S PROBABLY NOT THE DUST SHE'S ALLERGIC TO. TINY INSECTS, DUST MITES. THEIR BYPRODUCTS ARE ONE OF THE MOST COMMON ALLERGIES IN THE WORLD.
POOR BESS! DON'T WORRY, IT MAY NOT BE THE SORT OF MYSTERY I USUALLY SOLVE, BUT I PROMISE WE'LL FIND SOME WAY YOU CAN KEEP THEM!
THERE ARE ALL SORTS OF TREATMENTS, ACUPUNCTURE, IMMUNOTHERAPY SHOTS...
SHOTS?
OH, IT'S JUST A LITTLE PINCH IN YOUR ARM! NOTHING AT ALL! THEN YOU'LL SAY...
Don't miss NANCY DREW Graphic Novel # 6 – "Mr. Cheeters Is Missing"

Get a Clue!

Read

NANCY DREW

girl detective™

Smarter

Cooler

Quicker

Hipper

Surer

Braver

Faster

Newer

NANCY DREW girl detective

Super Mystery #2

ONCE UPON A ~~TIME~~... CRIME

A *New York Times* Bestselling Series!

Once Upon a Crime

Available wherever books are sold.

In *Once Upon a Crime*, Nancy has her own Cinderella-style adventure when she volunteers with a local charity to help build a community center. But, soon she begins to suspect that someone is trying to sabotage the project! As Nancy's fairy-tale adventure starts to turn into a nightmare, she realizes it'll be up to her to help her fellow volunteers live happily ever after.

Have you solved all of Nancy's latest cases?

Framed

Dangerous Plays

En Garde

Pit of Vipers

The Orchid Thief

Look for a new mystery every other month—Collect them all!

Visit www.SimonSaysSleuth.com for more Nancy Drew

Aladdin Paperbacks • Simon & Schuster Children's Publishing • www.SimonSaysSleuth.com

WATCH OUT FOR PAPERCUTZ™

The publisher of graphic novels created just for YOU!

Find out more about the big brains behind Papercutz on page 98.

TOTALLY SPIES! is now a part of the Papercutz line of super-stars! Discover new secrets about your favorite secret agents on page 100.

Papercutz is also proud to present a special graphic novel, THE LIFE OF POPE JOHN PAUL II ...*IN COMICS*! For more details about this major event in graphic novel publishing proceed to page 103.

There's big news in store for NANCY DREW, GIRL DETECTIVE! The star of the best-selling series of Papercutz graphic novels is heading for Hollywood! We've got the inside story starting on page 105.

THE HARDY BOYS have been on a wild and crazy ride since their very first Papercutz graphic novel. Check out where they've been and where they're going on page 108.

Fans have suggested that the "Z" in Papercutz stands for ZORRO! See for yourself the amazing cast of characters Zorro has encountered in his series of Papercutz graphic novels starting on page 111.

Meet TERRY NANTIER and JIM SALICRUP – the comics-loving guys that started

PAPERCUTZ™

This is the amazing tale of two men, born days apart, who have devoted their lives to comics. Terry Nantier, is a pioneer in the world of graphic novels, who for over thirty years has published work by the greatest artists and writers in the world – Will Eisner, Milton Caniff, P. Craig Russell, Lewis Trondheim, and many more. His partner in this new project, Jim Salicrup, started in comics when he was a wee lad of fifteen years old, and went on to become one of the most successful editors in the field, editing top titles such as the X-Men, the X-Files, the Fantastic Four, Dracula, and many more, including Spider-Man # 1 – the best-selling Spider-Man comic of all time.

A few years ago, Terry observed that most comics publishers were ignoring a vast potential audience of tweens and teens and focusing too much on older long-time comics fans. Seeing this opportunity to create a new generation of graphic novels for a new generation of fans, Terry and Jim went to work at once to make their vision a reality. The plan was simple—cool characters, in great stories, published in full-color in a digest-sized format. The best parts of traditional American comics would be combined with the most exciting elements of Japanese comics (called manga).

But what should they call this new comics company? Sylvia Nantier, Terry's brilliant daughter, suggested the name, and *Papercutz* was born.

In 2005 the debut Papercutz graphic novels were published – NANCY DREW, GIRL DETECTIVE and THE HARDY BOYS, with new books following every three months. And right from the start, fans loved the Papercutz approach — the first NANCY DREW, GIRL DETECTIVE graphic novel went into three big printings in its first year!

To stay on top of everything that's coming your way from Papercutz, we've created this special bonus feature. Everything you see presented in these pages is available now at your favorite booksellers. To get even more up-to-date news, be sure to visit www.papercutz.com.

Terry and Jim want to thank each and every one of you for picking up this Papercutz graphic novel. Don't be shy— let us know what you think. After all, we're working hard to produce stories that are not only fun and entertaining – but also respect your intelligence. Send your comments to our Editor-in-Chief: salicrup@papercutz.com

Caricatures by Steve Brodner.

They're here! TV's sensational secret agents on Cartoon Network are now starring in their own series of full-color graphic novels from Papercutz! Each Totally Spies! graphic novel features two big adventures starring Clover, Sam, and Alex doing what they do best—having fun while foiling the schemes of the wildest and wackiest criminal masterminds!

Sam, Alex, and Clover are three High School girls who fight crime on an international scale as undercover agents for the World Organization of Human Protection – WOOHP! Stressful? Sure. Exciting? Totally.

CONFIDENTIAL PERSONALITY PROFILES

Codename: CLOVER

Clover is a shopaholic who is always ready for action. Clover acts on impulse rather than reflection — and she can't stop falling in love!

Athletic, agile, and strong, Clover is definitely gutsy and never thinks twice about getting into the thick of the action. She is always ready to teach the bad guys a lesson, even when she has absolutely no chance of defeating them.

TOP SECRET

Codename: SAM

The most mature member of the team, Sam is rational and logical.

A star pupil, Sam is capable of finding solutions to problems that require a cool head and extra brainpower. She's the one who knows how to keep things in perspective and always defuses conflicts in a practical way—whether in the classroom or out in the field.

TOP SECRET

Codename:
ALEX

Alex, the youngest member of the team, is also the most affectionate. She admires her older friends, Sam and Clover, enormously and is determined to place their relationships above all else.

Being the youngest, Alex is also a bit gullible. She's frequently fooled by the baddies... as well as by her friends! Fortunately, Alex is very good-natured and never turns it into a big deal.

Codename:
MANDY

Mandy is Alex, Sam, and Clover's worst nightmare. She is in the same class as our three heroines. Overly self-assured, pretentious, and opinionated, Mandy is a real pest. Whether she's trying to get involved with the girls' private lives or desperately trying to outdo them in order to look cool, Mandy is always around the corner just waiting to cause the girls trouble.

Codename:
JERRY

As the head of the international secret agent organization WOOPH, Jerry thinks nothing of whisking the girls away from their daily lives to send them off in hot pursuit of a crazy villain halfway around the world!

Both a mentor and an instructor, Jerry is a second father to the girls. He's always there to congratulate them at the end of a successful mission.

RIDES OF THE PAPERCUTZ STARS

The souped-up NPU 3000 is the ultimate spy car – or is it? Find out in Totally Spies! #1!

THE LIFE OF POPE
JOHN PAUL II
...IN COMICS!

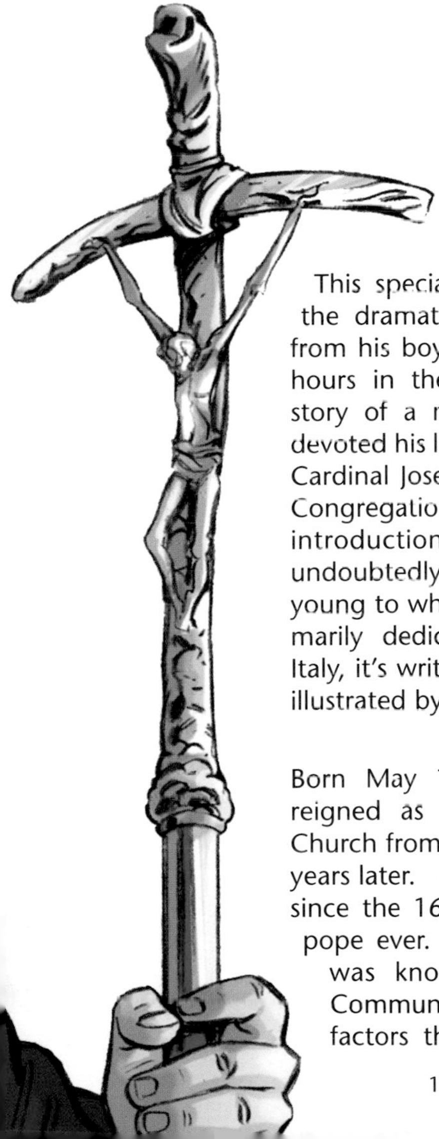

This special Papercutz graphic novel tells the dramatic story of Karol Wojtyla's life, from his boyhood in Poland to his sad final hours in the Vatican. It's the inspirational story of a man who loved humanity and devoted his life to his beliefs. As His Eminence Cardinal Jose Saraiva Martins, prefect of the Congregation for Saints' Causes writes in his introduction, the Pope's "message was undoubtedly understood foremost by the young to whom (this graphic novel is) ...primarily dedicated." Originally published in Italy, it's written by Alessandro Mainardi and illustrated by Werner Maresta.

Born May 18, 1920, Karol Jozef Wojtyla reigned as pope of the Roman Catholic Church from 1978 until his death, almost 27 years later. He was the first non-Italian pope since the 16th century and the only Polish pope ever. In his early years as pope, he was known for speaking out against Communism, and considered one of the factors that helped bring about its fall.

Even in his final years he was unafraid to speak out, and criticized contemporary greed in the forms of consumerism and out-of-control capitalism.

During his reign, the pope visited over 100 countries, more than any previous pope. While he was Pope the influence of the Church expanded in the Third World.

Pope John Paul II was well-loved worldwide, attracting the largest crowds in history. Attracting crowds of over one million people in a single venue and over four million people at the World Youth Day in Manila.

On April 2, 2005, at 9:37 PM local time, Pope John Paul II died after struggling with Parkinson's Disease, amongst other diseases, for many years. Millions of people flocked to Rome to pay their respects to the body and for his funeral.

This special Papercutz graphic novel is published at the larger 6" x 9" size, in full-color, as a jacketed hardcover, available at booksellers everywhere.

RIDES OF THE PAPERCUTZ STARS

The bulletproof Popemobile was created to protect John Paul II.

NANCY DREW GOES HOLLYWOOD!

Production commenced in Los Angeles on the live-action mystery adventure movie *Nancy Drew*, starring Emma Roberts (Nickelodeon's *Unfabulous*), Josh Flitter (*The Greatest Game Ever Played*), Max Thieriot (*The Pacifier*) and Tate Donovan (*Good Night, and Good Luck, The O.C.*) as Nancy's dad, Carson Drew. The movie is directed by Andrew Fleming.

In a published interview, Emma has revealed that she's "rather nervous because so many generations have read the books and I have big shoes to fill. But I'm really excited and it's going to be a lot of fun"

Nancy Drew is set to appear at the theater near you in August 2007, from Warner Bros. Pictures, a Warner Bros. Entertainment Company.

NANCY DREW Graphic Novel Episode Guide

Here's a great way to keep track of the Papercutz Nancy Drew, Girl Detective graphic novels...

Nancy Drew graphic novel #1
"The Demon of River Heights"
Stefan Petrucha, writer, and Sho Murase, artist
Join Nancy, along with Bess and George, as they search for missing student filmmakers and discover the deadly secret behind the local urban legend known as "The Demon of River Heights."

Nancy Drew graphic novel #2
"Writ In Stone"
Stefan Petrucha, writer, and Sho Murase, artist
It's double trouble for Nancy and her friends, when an ancient artifact and a little boy are both suddenly missing. Nancy's determined to recover both the artifact and little Owen, but someone's out to stop her – *permanently!*

Nancy Drew graphic novel #3
"The Haunted Dollhouse"
Stefan Petrucha, writer, and Sho Murase, artist
River Heights is celebrating "Nostalgia Week," and everyone in town is dressing up like it's 1930. But the fun is soon interrupted when the dolls in Emma Blavatsky's antique dollhouse seem to come alive and start depicting strange crimes that soon come true in real life. When Nancy stakes out the dollhouse, she witnesses a doll version of herself murdered!

Nancy Drew graphic novel #4
"The Girl Who Wasn't There"
Stefan Petrucha, writer, and Sho Murase, artist
Nancy receives a desperate call for help from Kalpana, her new friend in India. Soon, Nancy, along with Bess and George, are in New Delhi, looking for Kalpana, where not even Sahadev, a powerful crime lord, can scare Nancy off the case!

Nancy Drew graphic novel #5
"The Fake Heir"
Stefan Petrucha, writer, and Vaughn Ross, artist
Nancy Drew may have lost her ability to solve a mystery! It's totally embarrassing for Nancy to confront the very much alive Mr. Druthers — the man she claimed was murdered by his wife.

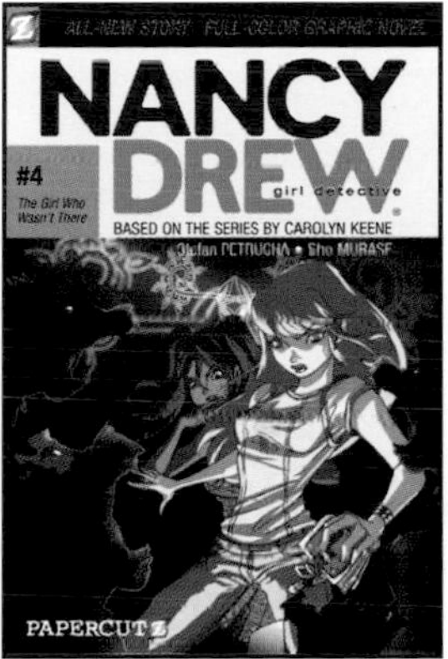

RIDES OF THE PAPERCUTZ STARS

Normally, Nancy Drew drives her gasoline-electric hybrid car, but she drove this roadster during Nostalgia Week.

THE HARDY BOYS®

Sam, Clover, and Alex, agents of WOOHP (World Organization of Human Protection), who are now battling the forces of LAMOS (League Aiming to Menace and Overthrow Spies), aren't the only spies lurking within the pages of Papercutz graphic novels! There was this guy, who Frank and Joe Hardy rescued in Hardy Boys graphic novel # 3...

The Hardy Boys ® Simon & Schuster

And, of course, Frank and Joe Hardy are now themselves under-cover brothers working for ATAC (American Teens Against Crime), the secret organization created by their dad, Fenton Hardy.

Recently, Papercutz Editor-in-Chief, Jim Salicrup had the pleasure of meeting Robert Vaughn, who played TV super-spy, Napoleon Solo on the classic The Man From U.N.C.L.E. (United Network Command for Law and Enforce-ment). Here the Man From Uncle checks out Hardy Boys graphic novel # 1, as The Man From MoCCA (Museum of Comic and Cartoon Art) looks on...

THE HARDY BOYS Graphic Novel Episode Guide

America's favorite undercover brothers star in an all-new, full-color series of Papercutz graphic novels, with all-new comics stories based on the series by Franklin W. Dixon.

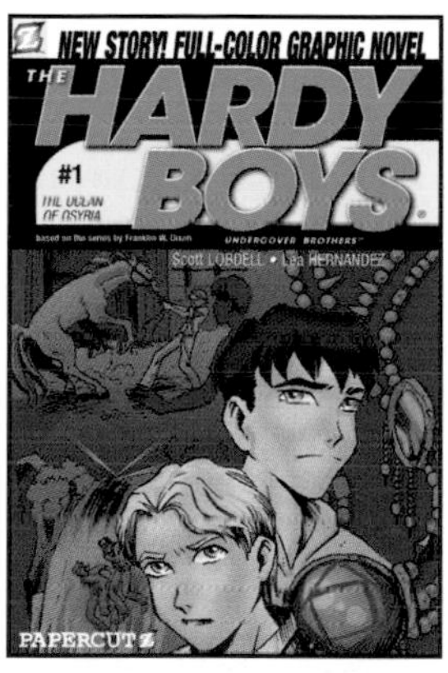

The Hardy Boys graphic novel #1
"The Ocean of Osyria"
Scott Lobdell, writer, and Lea Hernandez, artist
Frank and Joe Hardy, with Callie and Iola, search for a missing Mid-Eastern art treasure — "The Ocean of Osyria" — to free their friend, Chet Morton, who has been falsely accused of stealing it! It's like a blockbuster movie in comics form featuring your favorite teen sleuths!

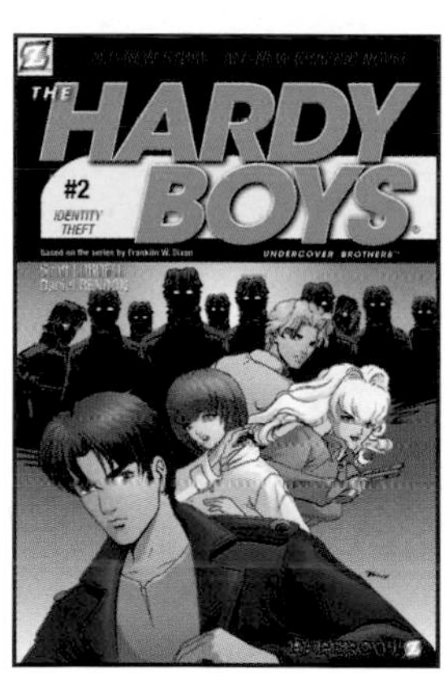

The Hardy Boys graphic novel #2
"Identity Theft"
Scott Lobdell, writer, Daniel Rendon, artist
Frank and Joe Hardy, are assigned a fantastic case of stolen identity — literally! Joy Gallagher claims another girl is now living her life, with her parents, and in her body! Is she insane? Or can her story actually be true? Featuring a special guest-appearance by Mr. Snuggles!

The Hardy Boys graphic novel #3
"Mad House"
Scott Lobdell, writer, Daniel Rendon, artist
Frank and Joe Hardy go undercover on the hit reality TV series "Mad House," the show in which contestants must live together in a house while cameras record their every move, to solve the mystery of who is harming the contestants— and why?! But things go from bad to worse when the Hardy Boys stumble upon a shocking murder!

The Hardy Boys graphic novel #4
"Malled"
Scott Lobdell, writer, Daniel Rendon, artist
Bayport's much-publicized new mall is about to open, but when suspicious accidents keep happening, ATAC sends Frank and Joe Hardy to investigate! The night before the Mall's Grand Opening, Frank, Joe, and eight others are mysteriously locked in the mall— with a murderer on the loose!

The Hardy Boys graphic novel #5
"Sea You, Sea Me"
Scott Lobdell, writer, Daniel Rendon, artist
The Hardy Boys get caught in a perfect storm! Frank and Joe go undercover aboard "the Silver Lining," an old fishing boat, to find out why teen crew members keep mysteriously vanishing. The number of suspects dwindles when one of the crew turns up dead!

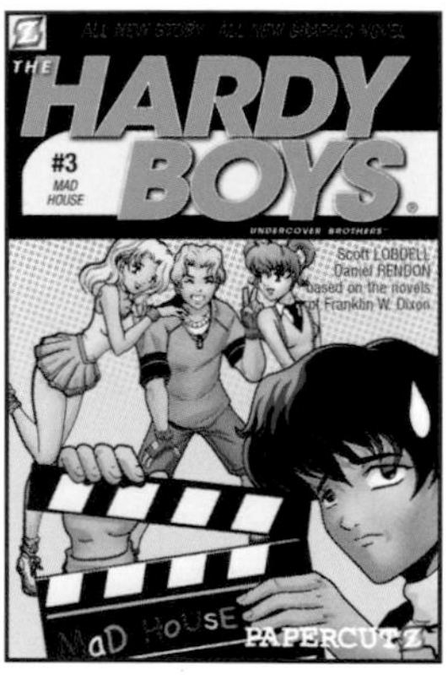

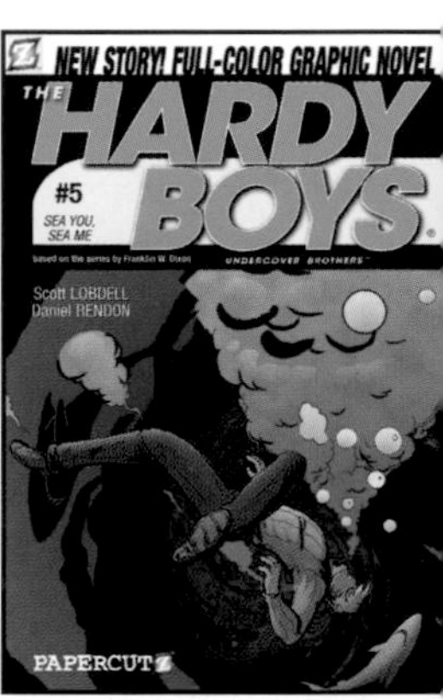

RIDES OF THE PAPERCUTZ STARS

Frank and Joe prefer motorcycles to cars.

The Papercutz Zorro graphic novels are unlike any other Zorro comics ever published before. The obvious difference is the Japanese comics style look of Sidney Lima's artwork. But the really big difference is that Zorro's new adventures take place outside of the pueblo de Los Angeles. Why would that community's legendary hero ever leave? The answer to that question is this woman:

Eulalia, risked her life to save Zorro from being shot by Commandante Monasterio. Enraged, he struck her across her face with his gun, scarring her, and sentenced her to death. Fortunately, Zorro has returned the favor, and rescued her before she could be executed. Now Zorro and Eulalia are on the run from Monasterio, who is determined to kill them both!

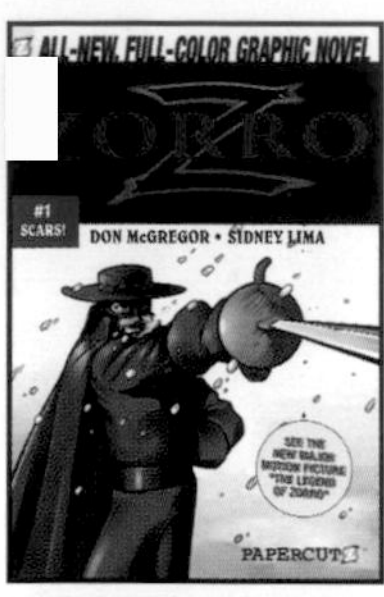

Zorro graphic novel #1

"Scars!"

Don McGregor, writer and Sidney Lima, artist

Zorro and Eulalia wind up in literally uncharted territory, and actually meet a mapmaker and his wife who are on the run from Lucifer Trapp, a man determined to keep this territory undiscovered at any cost!

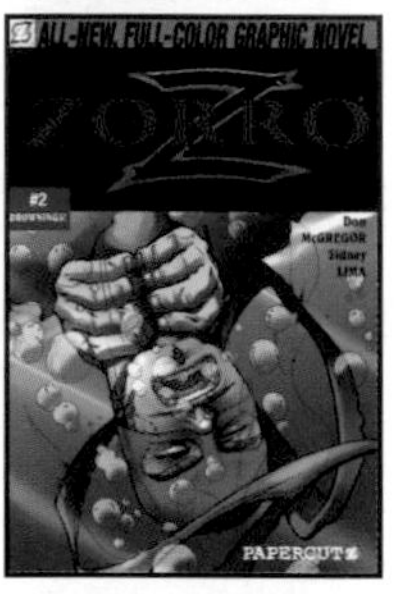

Zorro graphic novel #2

Don McGregor, writer and Sidney Lima, artist

"Drownings!" takes Zorro and Eulaia even farther away from Los Angeles, as they run into a couple fleeing the deadly Scorched Brothers. But after being with Eulalia day and night for several weeks, can Zorro seriously hope to keep his identity secret from Eulalia? What happens when Zorro is finally unmasked?

Zorro graphic novel #3

Don McGregor, writer and Sidney Lima, artist

"Vultures!" proves that wherever Zorro and Eulalia go, they are sure to encounter trouble! Zorro must save Normandie Caniff from becoming the next victim of a con artist called Lockspur. That's not easy to do when you're tied to stakes and being served up as dinner for ravenous vultures!

Will Zorro ever find a safe haven for the woman who saved his life? Or are they destined to be on the run forever?

RIDES OF THE PAPERCUTZ STARS

More than a means of transportation, the great black stallion, Tornado, is Zorro's friend.